Praise for the book

Daughter of Luharu is a compelling coming-of-age novel steeped in the history and social milieu of Pre-Independence India. With deep understanding and sensitivity, Monica Gupta gives readers a rare glimpse of rural Haryana – through the story of Roheeni, an unlettered woman who despite all the indignities she suffers, has the gumption to question her destiny and through that, challenge the perception of women in society. The story moves fast with many twists and turns, but carries an emotional, poignant undertone that makes it a captivating read!

Vinita Dawra Nangia
Executive Editor, *Times of India* and
Director, Times Literature Festival

In her first novel, *Daughter of Luharu*, Monica Gupta takes us back to the warmth of good old fashioned storytelling, the way grandmothers told us stories, the way folk tales were narrated, the way family secrets were passed down.

Rituparna Chatterjee
Author of *The Water Phoenix* and
Nawazuddin Siddiqui: An Ordinary Life

"Self-esteem is a fuel that can drive you through all your pain and miseries." Monica Gupta's *Daughter of Luharu* is a saga of empowerment that addresses the evils of our hypocritical patriarchic society which knowingly, unknowingly we all nurture.

It is a heart wrenching, gut punching tale of trials, tribulations and victories of innocence and the spirit of life.

Amol Kale
Film Maker

DAUGHTER OF Luharu

DAUGHTER OF Luharu

MONICA SUDHIR GUPTA

Vitasta

Published by
Renu Kaul Verma
Vitasta Publishing Pvt Ltd
2/15, Ansari Road, Daryaganj
New Delhi - 110 002
info@vitastapublishing.com

ISBN: 978-93-90961-50-4

First Edition 2022
MRP ₹ 399

Edited by Manjula Lal
Typeset & Cover Design by Somesh Kumar Mishra
Printed by Vikas Computer and Printers

To the kind and the courageous
To you, the mother and the daughter

Foreword

When Monica approached me to write the foreword for her book, *Daughter of Luharu,* I was overwhelmed by the honour because as an author myself I know what it takes to put your trust into someone with your book baby. The connection became even stronger when she told me that like my book, *Hiraeth - Partition Stories From 1947*, hers also had partition as the backdrop. Like me, she too has grown up on these stories and they have left a strong influence on us which is clearly evident in our choice of topic for our books.

Having said that, Monica's book goes beyond partition and is a story of a girl named Roheeni. Spanning over six decades, it traces her entire life. All her characters are beautifully built up including Roheeni's Gandhian husband, Vishnu Das, her cruel mother-in-law or for that matter even her brother-in-law.

The book is an ode to the spirit of a little girl, with no formal education, who grows up to be a strong woman who stands up for herself and her daughter. India's freedom struggle and its partition form an interesting background narrative in the book and play a pivotal role in the protagonist's journey.

Based in a village called Luharu, located in Haryana

(erstwhile Punjab province) and is quite similar to the village that the author lived in as a young girl. The influence shows through in the vivid descriptions that are made even more authentic with the details and the dialect.

This is a story of rare courage and struggle that should keep the readers engrossed with its twists and drama. I congratulate the author for introducing us to Roheeni who may have been an ordinary woman but ushered change not just for her own kith and kin but for many more around her. I wish Monica and her book all the success they deserve.

Best wishes!

Dr Shivani Salil
Author
Hiraeth - Partition stories from 1947

ACKNOWLEDGMENT

My heartfelt gratitude to my family and friends for their support, love and indelible faith in me. When I was researching for this book, it was the elders in my family who helped me out immensely by sharing their life experiences and anecdotes. I will be ever grateful to them for their input.

Thank you, Amrita Mukherjee, my dear friend for the numerous brainstorming sessions and expert feedback on writing skills. I owe you Amrita!

Rachna Gupta, your review at many stages helped me beat self-doubt. Thank you so much for your timely assurance.

A big thank you to Renu Kaul Verma for having faith in my work, to the entire team of Vitasta Publishing for making the book a better version of itself. You all rock!

Thank you Sudhir Gupta and my boys, Anant and Vivaan for keeping me motivated with your pampering and praises.

CHAPTER 01

The stairs were steep but I was used to running up and down a hundred times a day. All I had to do was press my palms on the uneven brickwork of the walls on either side. So when I started the ascent earlier in the day, I got a surprise.

The bricks weren't visible anymore. Instead, the walls were smooth to a fault. My olfactory nerves picked up the pungent smell of a fresh coat of paint. I liked this newness of my home. It had transformed completely in the last few days.

The renovation was a bit unsettling too. I missed the familiar fragrance that had enveloped me like a cocoon. There was something strange about this sparkling recentness. My home felt like a trap of revelations at every corner, every nook. Probably it was preparing me for the bigger surprise in my life.

'How will I go up the stairs?' I thought for a moment.

Then I spotted the rope, a thick one made from coconut husk. It was meant to be the banister. It looked neat, like everything else about my refurbished house. I clutched the rope to climb up. Then I realised I didn't really need any extra support. My strong limbs carried me easily up the stairs.

Sometimes you don't need support to achieve a goal. But you won't know unless you try.

'No one will walk beside you all the time. You will have to find your own way.'

Isn't that what Bibi always says?

The balcony I came to opened to eight rooms. Ours was the largest *haveli* (mansion) in Luharu but I had no clue about that until Bibi told me.

Everyone else called her Chand Bibi. I should have called her 'Tai' but I found Bibi more endearing. From the time I could utter a few words, I had called her Bibi. She liked it. I liked it. So for me, she was always Bibi.

'You don't know what you've got, Roheeni,' she used to say.

'You will be the owner of the largest house in the entire village.'

Her eyes weren't gleaming like they did when she talked about the times the Mughals held sway over India. I loved to hear stories of Akbar and Birbal from her. She told me about the Taj Mahal.

'It's an architectural wonder. Agra is not too far from Luharu. Maybe, you'll visit one day,' she would say.

I looked at the patterns on the floor, created by the sunlight streaming through the *jaali* in the walls. I wondered if the sunlight could do that in the Taj Mahal.

'Is the Taj Mahal as big as our *haveli*?' I asked Bibi curiously.

She laughed. 'I have heard it's really big—much, much bigger than this house.'

My imagination faltered. I hadn't been outside my home much, except for the trips to the market or the *mandir*. My imagination was limited to what I saw there. The grandeur of the Taj was beyond me.

'The Mughals have given India such a rich tapestry of art, music and architecture but look at us today,' she would say wistfully.

Did I notice that wistfulness in her eyes when she said this *haveli* will be mine? But I brushed the thought aside. Why would she be pensive about my good fortune? She loved me a lot. If someone really loved me, it was Bibi.

The large airy room I walked into was where Bibi and I had our endless post-lunch conversations. The room knew our secrets as well. We had a few, I must say.

The most important of them was Amreen. The first time I saw him, I couldn't look at Bibi for two days. It was harrowing to see her son lying on the cot. Bibi said he could never get up from bed unless the *jinns*, whom she invoked often, cured him.

He was twelve years old and the *jinns* had done nothing so far. He lay there staring at the broken ceiling of that one-room house. He could speak a few words, mostly muffled.

On that first visit, the stench of urine had nauseated me and the stark contrast of Bibi's poverty and my affluence had hit me like a boxer's punch.

Now I knew why all of Bibi's hair had turned grey at forty. Life had sprung a nasty surprise on her ten years back. The cholera epidemic that hit Luharu had taken away her husband and two of her sons.

'If I had the money, we could have bought medicines,' she rued often during our secret conversations.

Through her veil of tears, she looked at the desolate courtyard of our *haveli*. She looked longingly at the back door that opened up to other houses in the *mohalla,* as if it provided an escape route from her poverty.

Those affluent homes could never be hers, although she could work in one. She did more than her assigned jobs for our household. Her hardships and frustrations never came in the way of her affection for me.

The climb up the stairs had left me panting. I settled on the bed next to Bibi. The large bed had been shifted to a corner so that the paint on the walls could dry faster.

From where Bibi sat, she had a view of the *aangan* (courtyard), which was not its usual solitary self today. It was brimming with activity. Bibi was keeping a hawk-like watch on all that was happening.

'The *halwai*s have almost finished,' she said with authority, meaning the caterers had prepared the food.

I sprawled on the bed on my stomach and looked down through the arched window, my feet oscillating in the air, the *ghaghra* (long skirt) nonchalantly slipping down to my knees. I could be myself with Bibi.

My eyes followed Bibi's gaze. There were five of them working deftly by the giant *kadhai*s (woks). They had made batches and batches of *imarti*, *laddoos, mathadi, bhujia* that had all been stacked in the store rooms in the other wing of the house.

Our house actually had twenty rooms–big and small–and I was not allowed to enter all of them. I was definitely not allowed into the *kotha* that served as the storeroom for the newly-made sweets and sacks of grain, sugar, jaggery and spices.

'I can smell the roasting of *atta* in *ghee*,' said Bibi, inhaling deeply.

I sat up. The crisp smell of the *gund laddoo* roasted in ghee wafted through the *haveli* and I'm sure, like me, everyone else was salivating.

Bibi understood what was on my mind.

'Go and get some,' she told me.

'I can't. I am not allowed in the *kotha*,' I said.

'Maybe you could get some for Amreen too,' she said, her mischievous eyes twinkling.

That name was a catalyst. I instantly complied.

Amreen's name didn't evoke the picture of a broken ceiling and the stench of urine in my mind anymore. Instead, it painted the picture of a smile that would curve in a lopsided mouth as I would hand him the *gund laddoo.*

'What if I get caught? The house is teeming with people. It would be so embarrassing,' I said, on second thoughts.

'You are forgetting there is another entrance to the *kotha*. Just take the back door, no one will notice,' chuckled Bibi.

This was not the first time I was involved in a surreptitious activity with Bibi egging me on. I had done it before. I had smuggled out grains, dry fruit, pickles and *papad* from the *kotha* before, all for Bibi and Amreen.

I ran down the stairs without using the rope and patted myself on the back for my balance and confidence. I was standing behind a pillar wondering how to make myself inconspicuous when someone called.

'*Beti*, come see what lovely fabric they have here,' said Tai, my next door neighbour.

The allure of the beautiful fabrics was magnetic. I forgot about the sweets for a moment. These Muslim ladies, whom we called *janani,* were exquisite artisans. Their embroidered *odhani*s were to die for.

My eyes landed on a black one with gold embroidery, but before I could say anything Tai said in a rebuking tone to the *janani*, 'Why have you chosen a black one? Don't you know it's *manhoos* (inauspicious) for us (Hindus)?'

The *janani* quickly removed it apologetically from the *khaat* where the showcasing was being done and put it in her large fabric sack. I instantly lost interest and started retracing my steps.

'*Beti*, where are you going? Don't you like this orange one?' asked Tai.

'I'll go and get Bibi; she'll choose for me,' I said.

Instantly everyone stiffened.

'No, you can't ask her to come here,' said Tai urgently.

'Why?' I asked surprised.

'You just can't,' said Tai.

'Array, koeyna, bata de. (It's ok. Tell her)' said another lady, a neighbour of mine.

Tai looked hesitant.

The lady said, 'Bibi can't come because she is a *vidhwa* (widow).'

The *jananis* who were showcasing the cloth looked up, uncomfortable.

Like me, they had questions in their head but no one dared to ask.

'I'll come back,' I said and disappeared behind a pillar.

At this time of day, usually it was only me and Bibi in the house. Maybe, a couple of servants too, working silently in the kitchen. I revel in solitude.

***

Having fifty people running around the house is giving me the jitters. Everyone is busy. No one seems to have a moment to spare. The painters are putting the finishing touches on the walls, the women are buying clothes, men are bringing in the *anaaj* and the *halwai*s are churning out mountains of sweets.

The *halwai*s remind me of my real mission. I sneak into the other wing of the house, go up the stairs and then to the back door. It's locked. But I know where the keys were.

I run to a room on the same floor. The room looks spartan with only a bed and two large almirahs in one corner. I walk in and look under the mattress. The key is there.

I turn around and the key goes flying from my hand and lands on the floor. I hadn't heard him coming and bumped right into him.

I turn a crimson red, not daring to look into his eyes. They are usually kind, but I don't dare to see his expression now.

'Sit down on the bed,' he commands.

Trembling, I obey.

He sits next to me and takes off the white cloth wound on his head as a turban.

I glance sideways. His white *dhoti-kurta* look spotless as always. Will he hit me? But he has never done that.

When he places his hand on my head, I heave a sigh of relief. I have never seen my father getting angry or shouting at me, or for that matter at anyone else.

Nor is he someone with whom you could have a chat. He's a very quiet person. Whenever we are together, there are usually awkward silences between us. More is left unsaid than is ever said.

I fervently hope he would treat my folly with silence and would just let me go.

Instead, he chooses to speak.

'Why does Seth Janak Das' daughter need to steal his keys?' he asks.

I feel like just holding on to his index finger,

something I have always done whenever I need direction in my life and want to walk out of the room behaving like nothing has happened.

I can't stop the tears. I feel guilty, ashamed.

In a feeble voice I answer: 'I wanted to take some sweets from the *kotha*.'

'Who asked you to get it, Chand Bibi?'

I look up stunned. There are times Bauji has this uncanny ability to look through things.

I nod in the affirmative. There's no point lying to him now.

'But I want to have the sweets too,' I quickly add, trying to stand up for Bibi.

Bauji looks at me quizzically. Sometimes I feel he knows something about Bibi that I don't know.

'Don't you think it is funny that you are stealing in your own house?' asks my father.

On the rare occasions he speaks, I don't understand what he says most of the time because of the philosophy with which he often laces his words.

Like now. What does he mean?

'Roheeni, you have to understand all this is yours. This house, the money I have from my *vyapar* (business) and all the *halwai*s are preparing the sweets for you, for your wedding tomorrow. So you are like the princess now. All you need to do is ask and it will come to you. Why would you need to steal it?'

In my entire desolate existence, I had never felt like a princess. So what my father was saying felt like words spoken to another girl, in another universe.

'Always remember, our insecurities often make us cunning and we feel we are being smart. But honesty is what you need and self-confidence is what will take you far.'

I was lost again in his verbiage. What does he really mean? Self-confidence, insecurity, wedding, are not really words that hold much meaning to me. At eight years, does he really expect me to understand all this?

CHAPTER

02

My life, so far, has vacillated between great fortune and extreme misfortune. No one told me that to my face but I figured it out. This understanding left me with a sense of emptiness that an entire *kotha* of sweets, an elaborate wedding trousseau, or the prospect of having a handsome husband at the age of eight, could not fill up.

My father is now jingling the keys in his hand. He looks at me with warmth. He has never stared at me like that before. His eyes are always kind, but have a faraway look that I can't comprehend. It's like he's always looking at me with the intention of looking away.

This is a rare moment of closeness. I don't know how to react. I quickly hold his hand, more precisely his index finger. That finger was my comfort zone, my sense of security. I avoid his eyes, but the finger gives me solace.

'Now you will hold on to your husband's finger and

go only in the direction he points at,' says my father as he withdraws his hand to open the doors of the *kotha*.

Does marriage mean my father will not hold my hand again? The thought frightens me. Bibi told me that I will have a new home, a husband and a mother even. More than having a husband, the thought of having a mother excites me.

For the first time in my life, I would have a mother. I hoped she will oil my hair, braid it and give me a bath like all the mothers of the village did for their daughters.

'Don't expect that, Roheeni. You will be disappointed then. She is your mother-in-law; she will teach you a whole lot of other things and will definitely not give you a bath,' Bibi had said.

'Will she sleep with me?'

Bibi laughed. Her raucous laughter always sucked me in. I also started laughing without realising what was so funny.

Deep inside, those lonely nights had left a strange vacuum in my life. I had to deal with the looming, swaying neem tree that cast strange shadows on my bedroom walls. There were times I became jealous of Amreen, because he had Bibi with him at night; I only had my fear of ghosts and the big sprawling bed to myself.

When I was very small, a maidservant slept on the floor but as I grew up, I was alone. I sometimes expressed my nightly worries to Bibi, but she very conveniently brushed them aside because she wouldn't be able to do anything about it, least of all leave Amreen to be with me.

That's why maybe she understood why I wanted to sleep with my mother-in-law in my *sasural*, but chose to laugh instead. Or was there something that I didn't understand? I must admit the thought of sleeping alone in someone else's home is intimidating. That's the only thing I really fear in the new place. My home is a secure place. Despite the repairs and renovation, the decorations and the sudden invasion of the neighbours, it's my home. I had even ventured inside the *kotha* before, although Bauji didn't know about this.

He now unlocks the *kotha* door and is laughing. My hyper excitement at seeing the heaps of sweets inside the storeroom is the reason for his mirth.

'You can take some for your friends too,' he says.

'Friends?' I look at him surprised.

'Why? You don't have any friends? Wouldn't they come to the wedding?'

We live in the same house but I sometimes feel he knows almost nothing about me. Asking me to feed my dolls, who are getting married the same day, would have been more appropriate.

I have no friends. I never got a chance at friendship. I don't exactly know why, but girls of my age ignore me. They play *Ikka-dukka* and *Gitte* in the gulley but my attempts to approach them on a couple of occasions met with stony silence.

Only once did a girl speak.

'My mother says it would have still been okay if you had been born a boy. But you were born with all the bad luck. It was to give birth to you that your mother died. So we should keep away from you,' she announced.

Bibi told me that 1919 was the year when the maternal mortality rate at Luharu was really high. She didn't remember the exact statistics, but a number of women had lost their lives in childbirth. Some babies were never born, some were fortunate to be born males, while I…guess I was as unfortunate as my father. If only I had been a boy, his woes would have ended. But the death of my mother not only made him a widower for the third time, he was left with a girl to bring up.

As I said earlier, I was greatly fortunate because I was born to Seth Janak Das, the most hard-working and rich trader in the Baniya community in Luharu. My father owns stretches of land that roll into the sky. Hundreds of people work for him on this land. He also trades in textiles and grains.

The death of my mother with my birth meant all hopes of a male heir were dashed forever. Sadly, I was born with a fate that I couldn't change. As a girl, I couldn't have ruled over his vast kingdom.

Who is more ill-fated, me or my father? We have everything, yet we have nothing. It is as if we are joined at the hip by this nothingness that we refuse to look in the eye. I feel responsible for his disastrous existence and he feels responsible for my motherless reality.

I know for a fact that many of our family members tried to convince my father to get married for a fourth time. They said he should get someone to look after me and have a male child too, but he did not relent.

He chose to give all his attention to his business, leaving early in the morning and returning late at night. When it comes to getting attention, my father's business is my direct contender to whom I lose hands down–always.

Business is the only thing he's enthusiastic about, otherwise he's reclusive. Like me, he doesn't have friends. He is deeply religious, going to the *mandir* every day.

Apart from Bibi, Bauji and Amreen, if I ever talk to anyone, it's Babba, the *pujari* at the temple. Despite being so busy with the *puja* and the *aarti*, he always answers my questions with a smile on his face.

I go to the *mandir* often, holding on to my father's index finger. While my father prays, I pester Babba with questions.

The entrance to the *mandir* has three curved arches. The two arches on either side of the main arch have extended areas that double up as a sitting space. The main arch leads to a courtyard with ornate pillars and then the main Ram-Sita mandir. It's a small temple but everyone in the village goes there to pray.

Babba and I often sit on a charpoy in the *aangan* and he talks to me with an affection that I miss in my father. Sometimes, I squeeze into the space below the arch at the entrance and play with my doll sitting on the extended platform. Babba sits under the other arch and it's like a quiz game we play. I ask the questions and he answers.

'Who's that, Babba?' I asked one day looking at the carving of a man and a woman on the temple wall.

'That's Bhagwan Vishnu and his wife Laxmi,' he said. 'She was a very devoted wife so she stayed near her husband's feet all the time. When you get married Roheeni, sit by your husband's feet, take care of him, listen to him and treat him like God.'

The words stayed in my mind. From that day the concept of marriage meant the devotion of a disciple to God. Like my father prayed and sat at God's feet for hours at the mandir, I thought I had to do the same with my husband when I got married.

So you can imagine how ecstatic I was when my father first told me that I was getting married to a man named Vishnu Das. I felt Babba was right; I was getting my own God to pray to and I would be his Laxmi, his most devoted disciple.

Bauji says my God would be good to me. I have never seen him. Bauji had exchanged *sawa rupaiya* (Rs 1.25) with Vishnu's parents, which meant that our wedding was finalised.

Bibi told me Vishnu Das was exactly eight years older than me. He dropped out of school at fifteen to help his father in his business. His father Radheshyam is a *Baniya* grocer and his mother Bhagwani Devi is from the Jat community.

When other boys his age were whiling away their time swimming in the village pond, he was busy learning the ropes of his father's business. I was wide-eyed when Bibi told me that Vishnu is one of the few literate boys in his village Chiriya.

He is popular in his village because of his bargaining and accounting skills. He helps the farmers earn a better price for their harvest from traders at *anaaj mandis* in bigger villages and towns.

'At a young age, he has earned a good reputation for his polished behaviour. He isn't like the loud Jats or the mean Baniyas, devouring the money of poor farmers. Your father has made the right choice for you, Roheeni. He will keep you happy,' said Bibi.

My mind was a whirlwind. I kept thinking if he had gone to school, would he allow me to go to school? Would my Vishnu Bhagwan allow me to sit in a class and learn to read books? Would I be able to read Ramayana, as Babba read at the temple and shared stories of Ram, Sita and Hanuman?

CHAPTER 03

It didn't matter to me that prior to my wedding, I hadn't seen my future husband. Whatever little information I had about him was good enough. I actually looked forward to my wedding for two reasons. One was to have a mother and the other was the faint possibility that I might join school.

As luck would have it, there were plenty of reasons to be aghast about my *sasural*. For starters, their house is but a hut compared to mine. They have four rooms for five people; I am the sixth one in the family. Apart from Vishnu and my in-laws, there is his brother Kishan and his sister Geeta.

Not that I care much about the number of rooms or the size of a *haveli*. The rooms in my house served as my playground and home for my innumerable dolls. But the size of a house is supposed to matter to Seth Janak Das' daughter.

That was what I had overheard in a conversation the *tai*s were having.

'Her father is doing everything to ensure that she gets the same comfort in her *sasural.* He has got their house renovated and painted too,' said Sneha Mami, my maternal uncle Pramod Mama's wife.

'Two maids, one *dai* and one cook would make that four-hour long journey with Roheeni in a bullock cart to Chiriya. Imagine her mother-in-law's good luck. She won't have to lift a finger for anything,' said Sneha Mami.

The ladies sitting around Sneha Mami listened in rapt attention.

'How long would these people stay in her *sasural*?' someone asked.

'Till she can take care of things herself, that's what I heard Janak Das saying,' said Mami.

'He has sent them so many things; furniture, food, clothes, everything possible. After all, this is Seth Janak Das' daughter's wedding.'

'But poor man, he would not be able to do the *Kanyadan* (giving away of the bride),' said Binna Tai, a distant relative.

'Yes, he has bestowed the responsibility on me and my husband,' said Sneha Mami proudly.

'True, as a widower, he can't do *Kanyadan*. This ritual has to be done by a married couple. He is really unlucky. Became a widower thrice in his life,' said Binna Tai.

'*Chup*, Binna! Stop talking about all these things, especially today.'

Sneha Mami tried to silence Binna Tai and quickly looked around hoping no one had heard them.

Mami looked embarrassed when she spotted me trying to blend into the darkness of the *rasoi*.

'Arrey, Roheeni, you are not ready yet! The *Khoriya* dance will start soon and then the *Thaapa* ceremony will take place. Run up quickly and tell Bibi to get you ready,' said Sneha Mami.

I ran up the stairs totally puzzled about why my father wouldn't do the *Kanyadan* when I was his daughter. But I didn't get a chance to ask Bibi, because she was already waiting with my *ghaghra-angia* and an *odhani* with elaborate Phulkari designs on it. I tried to see my face in the small mirrors that were stitched into the cloth with colourful threads of bright orange, yellow, red, green and blue.

It was definitely more elaborate than the regular cotton *ghaghra-odhani* I usually wore. And I found the tiny mirrors more mesmerising than the newly installed full-length one in my room. Bibi had partitioned off a part of the extended terrace with sarees and bed sheets, so that I could get my ablutions done there.

Our bathroom was far away on the other side of the *aangan*. I wished it was right inside my room but you could not have something as impure as a latrine inside the house. So I had to wake up at 5 am to make that long trip across the courtyard because the whole household woke up after that during those busy days of my wedding ceremony.

There were loud sounds of *dholak* and singing. The

Khoriya dance, in which women mime the entire wedding ceremony, was about to begin. I had taken part in it at other people's weddings. Dancing with them was really enjoyable. This was the only time women could dance at a wedding because they weren't allowed to do so when the men danced at the *baraat* procession.

Before Bibi knew it, I had walked out from behind the saree curtains and I was standing by the *jharoka*, the window looking out to the road, to catch a glimpse of the dancers' arrival.

Bibi was shouting, 'Roheeni! Roheeni! Have you gone mad?'

She dragged me inside the room and closed the door shut with a loud bang.

'Put on your clothes! Never do this again. What will people at your *sasural* say? They will say I have not taught you anything, your father has not taught you anything. Allah! Put some sense into this girl's head.'

I couldn't make out what the whole issue was. I was used to wandering around naked in my own quarters. There wasn't anyone there anyway, except Bibi.

Bibi came to me with the *angia*. I jumped on the bed. I wouldn't give in to clothes so easily. I wanted to play a game with Bibi. She had to catch me first.

As I ran around the room, I caught a glimpse of myself in the mirror. A child stared back at me. A child who wanted to have some fun at her own wedding, like her dolls had at theirs.

But Bibi was clearly in no mood for fun. Her robust

frame was no match for my tiny, sprinting body. One round around the bed and she was already panting. Then she did something totally out of character.

She grabbed my hair and pulled me down. My scalp hurt and I winced.

'Never do this again,' she hissed. Her wide eyes looked menacing.

I started crying.

I sat soberly through the *Khoriya* dance ritual. My tight-fitting *angia* gave me a violent itch, but I didn't dare to slip in my fingers inside the blouse for relief.

The women sang, '*Lado! Beti ka baap sada hina*. (A girl's father is always a loser).'

It was a traditional song popular at weddings in villages in our area, I had heard it before. But in my case, it seemed to have a whole new interpretation.

I looked at my father, who was sitting with the men with the usual distant look in his eyes. I wanted to ask him: Do you really think you are a loser because you had me?

The glitz at the wedding surely made me feel he wasn't. The whole haveli was decorated with fragrant flowers. People served food and drinks to all the guests. I sat in my heavy *odhani*, huge gold *malas* adorning my neck and a heavy gold *borla* sitting on my forehead.

Everyone said I looked beautiful. And I had to admit that was something I was told for the first time in my life. I felt like a winner, but why were they talking of my father losing out? But wait, they were not talking about my father. This song was meant for every father with a daughter in Luharu village. Wasn't it?

For the *Thaapa* ceremony, a drawing was made on the wall with *geru* (orange chalk) and our dead ancestors were invoked to bless the bride. For a fleeting moment, I thought my mother also came to see the daughter she could never hold. The daughter she wanted to bless nevertheless.

I was so lost in thought, I hadn't realised the *mehendi* ceremony had started. They were applying henna on my hands and feet. Now I would have to sit still. On top of that there was an itchy *angia* to deal with. There was no one with whom I could share my predicament. Bibi was still mad at me for my waywardness earlier in the evening.

But I felt there was something more. She didn't take kindly to the fact that I was caught red-handed by my father while stealing from the *kotha*. Then, my father had asked me to get the *boondi* while he talked to Bibi. I don't know what he told her but she had been sulking since.

She got her mojo back the next morning. She had to be on her toes to get me ready in time for the wedding rituals that were slotted one after the other. The *Pithi Dastoor* or *Haldi* ceremony was in the morning.

Just when Bibi bathed me to rub off all the sticky turmeric from my body, the *baraat* arrived. They came with a huge entourage of what looked like a hundred people. My father had made elaborate arrangements for them in the other wing of our haveli.

It was also time for my doll's *baraat* to arrive, so

like everyone else in my house I didn't care to occupy a vantage point next to the *jharoka* to get a glimpse of my groom.

During the wedding, I kept my eyes down, as Bibi had told me categorically and ensured I had a good look at my husband's index finger on the right hand. It was as shapely as my father's. But I didn't know how secure I would feel holding it tightly. I kept my eyes deliberately stuck to his hands, or to the *Tilli jutti* he was wearing. The *ghunghat* covering my head down to my chest didn't allow much more.

After the *Gath Bandhan* and *Pani Grahan* ceremonies, it was time for the *Kanyadan*. My father stepped aside as Sneha Mami and Pramod Mama did the *Kanyadan*. They hadn't eaten a morsel or even sipped a drop of water since morning, so that they could maintain the fast needed for the ritual. My father and I had eaten an elaborate *thali* for lunch.

I had enjoyed my last meal as a maiden in the haveli with my father. He even fed me with his hands—another first in my life.

He should have felt happy about it like I felt now. But he looked forlorn, was that a teardrop I spotted at the corner of his eye? My wedding made me aware of the emotions that my father had for me, something he hadn't ever shown when all those eight years passed by. Wasn't I there right in front of him—in his house, in his life?

After the *Pheras*, it was time for *Mahira Dastoor* where my maternal uncle, Pramod Mama, was supposed to give me gifts, expensive ones at that.

Mama gave me gold bangles called *hansils*, an elaborate gold *nath, malas* and expensive embroidered fabric. But I had seen Bauji buying the same things from the goldsmith. So I presumed it was my father who bought all the things that were passed off as Mama's gifts.

Of course, there was no way of confirming that because Bauji wouldn't be happy if I asked.

Once the wedding rituals were over, all the ladies took us – the bride and groom – to a room for *Jui Khilai*. The women asked him to find the gold ring inside a heap of rice. I found it before he did. But I didn't look up to see if I had angered him or he was smiling. My *ghunghat* had been drawn further down.

I felt so triumphant. I had beaten my husband at a game. Then I suddenly remembered what my father had said: My husband would lead and I would have to follow. I couldn't beat him at a game.

Vishnu Das won all the other games we played. I just kept my eyes fixed on his index finger.

'Now sit next to him,' said Sneha Mami. I don't know why all the women were suddenly giggling so much.

They asked me to sit next to him and feed him. But how could I? He was Vishnu and I was Laxmi. Hadn't Babba said if I had to be a devoted wife, I should sit at his feet?

I occupied a spot next to his feet. His hands were resting on his knees, his index finger was pointing downwards. I had finally got at least one thing right. I had learned to follow the direction of his finger. I was a good wife like Laxmi. But I hadn't seen my husband yet. The *ghunghat* didn't allow it.

CHAPTER 04

The *haveli* went back to its accustomed silence the next morning. Where had all the people gone? What happened to all that din and bustle that had accompanied my wedding preparations?

I guessed that with the rituals over, I had been left to my own devices. I started looking around the room for my dolls. I hadn't played with them for almost a week. I felt sad about neglecting them.

Sneha Mami entered the room.

'You are up?' she asked cheerfully.

'What do you want to eat?' she asked.

'*Imarti*,' I replied without thinking twice.

'How much more *imarti* will you have? You had eight last night, I think,' she said good-naturedly.

'Mami, where is everyone? The house is so silent,' I asked her.

'They have all gone to the *Sabha* (meeting). Even your *dulha* (groom).'

My groom had gone already? Was that alarming? And what was a *Sabha*?

Looking at my alarmed face, she quickly added, 'Don't worry, Roheeni, he took permission from your father and went. It's not every day you get to see Gandhiji.'

I had heard of Gandhiji. Bibi always said he would change the world for the better. He would make Muslims and Hindus live together as brothers and sisters.

'The *Khalifat* movement…didn't he have something to do with it?' I asked.

Mami looked at me wide-eyed.

'*Wah!* Roheeni, you know so much despite not going to school.'

I treated this as a jab, it wasn't really a compliment.

My jaws stiffened and I put on my know-it-all air.

'Yes, Bibi told me Gandhiji joined the *Khalifat* movement started by the Muslims to fight for freedom–*Swaraj*.'

Mami ignored me.

'You know, Roheeni you were born on the day the Jallianwala Bagh massacre happened in Amritsar: 13 April 1919.'

She managed to sprinkle salt on my already existing injuries. I had heard a thousand times about my connection to that ghastly massacre. There were times I wondered if I had actually engineered that massacre or my mother's death. I had wondered if there was some evil spirit lurking inside me that came to this earth in my baby form.

'Listen, don't tell anyone in your *sasural* that you were born on the day of the massacre,' said Mami.

She was talking in a whisper as if telling me not to spill a horrifying secret.

'I'll get you some *imarti.*'

She left but I remained troubled. Was there really something wrong with me?

Bibi entered the room. I breathed a sigh of relief. Bibi was home to me, my solace.

'Gandhiji has come and you didn't go?' I asked her.

'Who would dress you up for your *vidaai* then?'

'Even the *dulha* has gone there,' I giggled.

'For men, some things are more important than getting married. For women, life is only about responsibility. You will learn that with time,' Bibi said philosophically.

'What will I do without you there?' I suddenly burst out crying. Bibi held me tight. She was crying too.

'You will come back soon to visit me,' she said.

The distance from Luharu to Chiriya was four hours by bullock cart. We had to start off early to reach before the sun went down.

I was dressed up in a beautifully embroidered *angia*, a heavy *odhani-ghaghra*. The gold necklaces sat heavy on my chest which was already brimming with a sense of uncertainty.

Bibi told me she had been to Chiriya once and I shouldn't expect it to be anything like Luharu. It was a very small village and my *sasural* was probably the only *pucca* house in a lane of *kuccha* houses with straw roofs.

'Thc village has two wells and one large pond. I think you will have to go to the pond for your bath and for washing clothes,' said Bibi, while clasping the gold earrings.

'The servants will be there. Can they make a bath for me like you do?'

'Spoilt brat,' she laughed.

My father was sending two maids with me to my *sasural*. They would do all the washing, cleaning, cooking that a new bride was supposed to do post-wedding. I was supposed to take over when I was sufficiently trained by my mother-in-law.

So there were six bullock carts. One for me, one for the maids, one for two security guards and three for all the stuff that I was carrying from my *maika*: gold jewellery, clothes, gifts and sweets.

I was really excited about the bullock cart ride. I had been on one only twice in my life. Usually, I went to the *mandir* and market with my father and that was always on foot.

My father was standing next to the bullock cart with all the women–my relatives and neighbours–to bid me goodbye.

That reserved look in his eyes was back, the poignant expression that I had spotted on his face the evening before was replaced by the business-like persona of Seth Janak Das.

There was no groom waiting to take me home, he was doing more important things at Gandhiji's Sabha. The bullocks and the driver were going to be my companions. I didn't have a best friend so there would not be anyone sitting beside me in the bullock cart.

I clutched my father's finger and started crying. I didn't really know why I was crying. Was it because I would miss my father and my home or was it because of the uncertainty I felt about my future?

I was given a handful of rice and coins to throw over my head as I stepped out of my home. It was meant as a repayment of the debt I owed my father for bringing me up.

I embarked on the bullock cart ride. I looked up to see Bibi looking down at me from the *jharoka*. She wasn't allowed to bid me goodbye for the same reason she wasn't part of any wedding ritual–because she was a widow.

I looked away and took a deep breath. I focused my attention on the journey ahead.

This was a particularly hot summer. The sun was already beating down at 10 am. The thatched roof of the bullock cart provided some relief, but the zephyr trailing the vehicle made my lips dry.

The dust from the road whirled in the wind and aimed for my eyes. I pulled the *ghunghat* farther down. But I pulled it back again because I wanted to see the road I was taking. The lush green fields, the yellow mustard flowers dancing in the wind and the long winding road travelling to eternity. I couldn't take my eyes off this beautiful scene.

The beauty of my surroundings made me forget how lonely my journey was. The groom wasn't taking me home, I was travelling alone, unsure of my place in his busy life.

I think we had travelled an hour when I finally spotted men in white *kurtas*, *dhotis* and a weird white cap on their head that looked like an upturned boat.

Then there were some women in their bright cotton sarees and then there were more and more people walking down. The road that had looked so forlorn minutes ago became crowded. There were men, women, children and a few bullock carts, all going in the same direction as my entourage.

A point came when the dirt road meandered into the fields and everyone took that route. Our carts crossed that point and continued on the main road. I looked far into the field and it was brimming with people. There were probably hundreds of them. On a raised platform stood a number of men in those upturned-boat caps and in their midst stood a frail, bald man in a white *dhoti* that came to his knees and a white *chadar* over his upper body. I think he had specs on. He was talking and the crowd was listening in rapt attention.

The bullock cart moved on slowly, but I kept craning my neck to hold on to the receding scene.

Had I just seen Gandhiji? I wanted to run to Bibi and ask her. Then the reality hit me that I couldn't do that anymore. The dirt road had taken me far away from her.

CHAPTER 05

The warm breeze, the monotonous rhythm of the bullock cart and the silence of the road lulled me to sleep. In fact, dozing off seemed to be the best solution to the problem I was facing. Hunger and trepidation were creating strange ripples in my stomach; I thought maybe if I could catch forty winks, I could keep that feeling at bay.

I woke up when I heard the voices of children. I could make out they were running behind the bullock cart shouting, '*Dulhan aagi!* (Bride has arrived).'

I looked outside and struggled to catch a glimpse of the running children through my *ghunghat*. I did not dare to pull it back too much. Bibi had told me, doing that would be treated as sacrilege in my *sasural*.

They were running with the cart now. They were probably my age or even older. Suddenly I had this urge to jump down from the cart and run with them and look at the *dulhan* too. I wanted to share their excitement, their freedom, their unbridled laughter.

The dirt road entered an area where there were one-storey small houses with round mud walls and thatched roofs haphazardly lining the road. The colour of the road blended into the walls and gave the village a uniform texture.

The houses were interspersed with trees, clothes hung here and there and elderly people were sitting outside on charpoys as toddlers played around. This place was very different from the cobbled roads of Luharu. The houses were big there, made of brick and mortar, painted bright and all the activity was restricted to the *aangan*. That was where the charpoys were set, not outside the house.

As the bullock cart made its way through the road that had narrowed considerably after entering the village and the children kept shouting, announcing my arrival, women rushed out of their homes to see me.

Sensing their excitement, I suddenly felt very special. Attention was something I had craved for all my life and here I was being showered with it, without even asking for it.

I had this uncanny instinct to wave at everyone like a princess would when she passed through her kingdom and her people paid allegiance to her. I felt like flicking back my *ghunghat*, standing at the helm of the bullock cart and shouting, 'Here is your *Rani* Roheeni.'

The crowd kept expanding on both sides of the road

till it came to a point where the bullock cart had to stop because it could not penetrate the crowd. I looked to my right and saw a decorated door that possibly led to an *aangan*. The wall next to the door had a fresh coat of paint just like my own house.

I had heard Bauji telling Sneha Mami that my mother-in-law Bhagwani Devi was very happy about the renovations. I could now see why. The house stood out in the village.

Usually, a bride came to her *sasural* with the *baraat*. But in my case the *baraat* and even the groom had all gone to Gandhiji's *Sabha*, so I presumed they would arrive later in the day.

A group of women helped me inside the house and the two maids that my father had sent with me, Lajjo and Gulabi, followed.

The house had a large courtyard decorated with *rangoli* and there were rooms around it. It wasn't sprawling like my haveli, but it was big enough for me to breathe freely. I could smell fresh paint. It felt like home.

I was dying of hunger and wished they would serve me some food. I was served *lassi* and then asked to sit on a charpoy for the *Mooh Dikhai rasam*.

Bibi told me this was an important ritual, because the women weren't a part of the *baraat*, so they would only see the bride's face when she came to the *sasural*. They would also give me gifts.

Did they have *imarti*? I wished they had handed me one instead of gifts. I was starving.

I was a bit startled when one lady sat next to me and pushed back my *ghunghat*. I had by now become so used to pulling it down that having it pulled back worried me. Is this the right thing to do? I thought.

Looking at my startled face, the lady said gently, 'Won't you let your *saas* (mother-in-law) see your face?'

Saas? So this was my mother-in-law. I looked up at her dark kohl-lined eyes. The eyes looked bright, powerful.

Then I noticed her bloated belly. She looked just like all those women who couldn't move before they had babies.

So was my mother-in-law going to have a baby? The question in my head was answered quickly.

'Bhagwani, you are really lucky. You have a rich girl as a *bahu* who has come with two maids. Now in the last days of your pregnancy you won't have to move a finger. In fact, even after that,' someone said.

'And she is not lucky to be a bride to my Vishnu? You all know he is one in a million.'

My mother-in-law spoke proudly, looking at me all the while. She then turned my face once to this side, then to that side and ran her fingers through my hair, maybe to check my skin was blemish free and hair free of lice.

'She is darker than you,' another lady said.

My mother-in-law smiled, but chose not to answer.

Her fingers were caressing my gold ornaments now. I guess all the women of Chiriya had descended on the house. They were all talking at the same time, crowding around me and I was starting to feel hungry and claustrophobic. I wanted the ritual to end quickly.

I looked at Lajjo with pleading eyes. But she wasn't Bibi; she couldn't decipher my expression. She couldn't understand I wanted to be rescued.

'But she is a rich man's daughter; you will have a hard time controlling her. I am sure she comes with all the airs of a spoilt rich girl.' The voice came from the crowd. I couldn't lend a face to it.

'Our Roheeni isn't like that,' said my mother-in-law. 'She is a very good girl. Aren't you?'

I nodded.

'I want to see the new bride! I want to see the bride!' I heard an excited voice emerging from the crowd.

'Come Geeta, see your Bhabhi,' said Bhagwani Devi and she got up with some effort to give the girl her place.

Geeta sat next to me. She was my age or maybe a few years older. She was wearing the same Phulkari *odhani* that I was wearing; only the colour was different. It must have been a gift from my father.

She looked at me wide-eyed.

'You have brought so many things in the bullock cart. Ma, can I wear some of the gold jewellery?'

Everyone started laughing as if she had cracked the joke of the century. I didn't get the humour.

'You don't have to ask anyone, Geeta. Your Bhabhi's things are yours. Take whatever you want,' said my mother-in-law.

'I will take the dolls then,' jumped up Geeta.

My heart was in my mouth. My father had bought

me two new dolls. I wanted to tell her she could take all the jewellery and clothes, but the dolls…not the dolls, please. Those were mine. I wanted to play with them.

Geeta was gone. I hadn't spoken. The *Mooh Dikhai rasam* continued. An endless stream of women came, held my face by the chin, made remarks–some sounded nice, some sarcastic, some downright rude–handed me gifts and moved aside. I kept sliding into a daze. My hunger was getting the better of me now.

Geeta appeared again, holding my dolls in her hand this time.

'Ma, see my dolls,' she told her mother excitedly.

'They're all yours. Take whatever you want,' she beamed at her.

'But first take Roheeni inside.'

Geeta grabbed my hand. I almost stumbled on the long edges of my *ghaghra*. She took my hand and led me to a door on the side of the *aangan*. It had fresh green paint on it.

Lajjo and Gulabi were behind me.

'Not you,' said my mother-in-law gruffly.

I was puzzled.

'Low caste Ahir women cannot enter the house,' she said with finality.

My mother-in-law was Jat and father-in-law was Baniya like me and I knew Ahirs were low caste. But in my home in Luharu, there was no such rule for low caste women. They all worked inside the house.

'I will get someone to show you your living quarters,'

said Bhagwani Devi.

The maids stepped back and I stepped inside a room that smelt of new furniture and varnish. My eyes rested on the beautiful wooden headboard. It had two peacocks facing each other carved in the wood. There was a dressing table with the same design of two peacocks on both sides and the birds were there on the gigantic wooden almirah too, that stood in a corner.

I was taken aback by the lavishness it stood for. I had never seen such beautiful furniture. My own home was rather sparsely furnished.

'The *kaarigars* your father sent worked on this furniture for months,' said Geeta.

'They made a wooden doll's house for me. You want to see?'

'I'm hungry,' I finally uttered the words.

Geeta started shouting, 'She is hungry! She is hungry!'

She left the room holding the dolls by their hair. My eyes trailed them wistfully.

I needed to use the bathroom too. It had been more than five hours since I had left home.

But I felt scared if I told Geeta, she would shout that out too, in the same way she talked about my hunger.

Finally, I told my mother-in-law, still not sure how she would react.

Thankfully, she just smiled and sent me off with Gulabi and another lady to the back of the house. A dirty *naala* (open drain) was flowing at the back.

'This *naala* is for kids and older women. We go

behind those bushes,' said the lady, pointing to a bush at a distance. I gulped. Was I expected to walk that far?

'But since she is the new bride, she can use the *naala*,' the lady said.

I gulped again. The *naala* smelled nauseating. I was supposed to squat over it.

But my urgency was too much and my bladder was revolting. I shut out the smell and let myself go.

I felt very angry at my father. He had done everything to this house, but not for once thought how his daughter would feel using the *naala*. Couldn't he have constructed a latrine next to the *aangan*?

A large silver plate with a heap of *puris* and *kheer* was presented to me. I was hungry alright, but did they really expect me to eat so much?

I started on the plate with the determination that one started to fight in a war. I had to win.

But I wasn't quite prepared for the enemy that was sitting right on my head–my *ghunghat*. Holding the *ghunghat* in place with the left hand and reaching the food to my mouth with the right hand was an effort that exasperated me.

It might have been an hour or maybe even more, but at the end of the struggle not a single morsel was left on the plate, although I felt I had grown a belly like my mother-in-law's.

All the while I ate, my mother-in-law kept fanning me with a hand fan telling me how I was a lucky bride because I had Vishnu Das for a husband.

Not for a moment did she ask about me. I was happy, though. I always felt my identity was tangled with my deceased mother and that was why I was never comfortable talking about myself.

And even if she had asked, what would I have said?

I had never gone to school, I didn't have friends, I didn't know how to cook, wash or clean or for that matter do any kind of housework. And my mother had died because of me.

'Oh, I should have told you to remove the *ghunghat* and eat. We are all women here anyway. It just never struck me,' said my mother-in-law.

I didn't know that this was the beginning of my learning process about the ways of Bhagwani Devi. For now, a sense of unpredictability surrounded this lady.

There was commotion outside. Someone said the *baraatis* were back. That meant I would have to pull down my *ghunghat* again. I was told in front of every man, even at home in front of my father-in-law, I should keep my *ghunghat* down. It felt so constricting. I couldn't see anything with the *ghunghat* drawn.

But a burp threatened to come up and make a noisy exit through my throat. I couldn't push it down; it came as fast as this man entered the room.

I burped loudly right in front of him. I was so embarrassed I forgot to pull down my *ghunghat*. So I gaped at him.

He was tall and fair. He was wearing that upturned-boat white cap like everyone else at that Sabha. He was a very good-looking boy.

I pulled down my *ghunghat* quickly.

My mother-in-law started laughing.

'You don't have to do that in front of your husband,' she said.

Husband? So this was my husband. This was Vishnu Das. I desperately wanted to catch another glimpse of him but felt too shy to pull back the *ghunghat*.

'Can you imagine I got to see Gandhiji?' he said excitedly to Bhagwani Devi.

He behaved like I did not exist, as if I was not present in the room. I felt more invisible in my *sasural* than I had felt in my home.

CHAPTER 06

One good thing about being married is that I don't have to sleep alone anymore. But I don't sleep on the ornate bed that my father had got made for me. That room largely stays empty.

On some afternoons, Maji and my father-in-law Radheshyam Das have a siesta in that room after lunch. Some days I see Geeta playing with her dolls there but I am somehow not allowed into that room.

'This room is for the elders,' Maji told me after a few days of marriage when I was about to enter seeing Geeta playing there.

If it had been Bibi, I would have probably tried to be funny saying, 'Is Geeta an adult then?'

But at my *sasural*, I have learned to keep my mouth shut, otherwise there will be consequences. I do want to sleep on that ornate bed but never express my desire. If my mother-in-law feels I am not listening to her, that could mean fetching three more pails of water from the village well, or grinding more wheat at the *chakki* or going without food for a day.

My life hasn't panned out exactly the way I believed it would in my *sasural.* Fantasy and reality rarely match. I had hoped I could play with Geeta all day with the dolls and at night my husband would read out books to me. Then I would tell him that I wanted to go to school and he would immediately oblige.

I was sure Lajjo and Gulabi would do all the work and I would prance around the house most of the time, as I did in Luharu. I hadn't actually paid much heed when Bibi told me that I would get all my training from Maji. A few months into my marriage, I know what she meant.

There are three charpoys in our room. One is mine. In the other two, Geeta and Maji sleep. I am used to having a double bed to myself, but willing to trade that comfort for some company at night.

Geeta would keep whispering this and that and then she would suddenly stop talking and I would find her fast asleep. As the night progresses, the light snore of my mother-in-law along with the heaving of her distended stomach feel strangely reassuring.

My father-in-law, my husband and my brother-in-law Kishan sleep in the *aangan,* the breeze lulling them to sleep. I wish I could enjoy a bit of the cool breeze outside but in our household, women are strictly not allowed to sleep in the open.

In many ways, my father-in-law Radheshyam Das is like my father. He speaks very little, is out of the house most of the time, but there is something he has which my father doesn't. He has a temper. And he shows that temper if he feels the *phulka*s served to him are not direct from the oven. He hates food that is not piping hot. He can bring the house down because of that.

He is small and thin when compared to my robust, fair-skinned, pretty mother-in-law but he makes up for his size with his temper.

He never speaks to me and I realise I am largely Bhagwani Devi's responsibility. My husband also feels that way. He does give me spurts of attention that I thoroughly enjoy. But the attention comes only when I am in dire straits.

My day starts when the village rooster announces the advent of dawn. I had to learn how to milk the cow. On the first day, I was really enthusiastic because we never had any cows in our house in Luharu. Fresh milk was delivered to us by the milkman every day.

When I went to the cowshed, I was really excited. There are four cows and a calf in the shed lined with straws. Maji led me to the cow that was the mother of the calf and told me it would be easier to milk her.

But she seemed a bit jittery around me and kept moving as I tried to sit next to her udder with the pail pressed between my legs.

'Hold like this and pull,' said Maji.

It looked easy but I soon realised it wasn't. The cow

wouldn't stand still and it kept kicking. Every time I got a grip of the udder and pulled, it kicked and moved away.

I could feel Maji's growing impatience. She showed me a couple of more times but I couldn't do it.

'This is what happens if you get a rich girl as your *bahu*. She is as worthless as those Ahir women she has brought along with her.'

The blood shot up to my ears and made my face red with shame; her eyes too had turned crimson with rage.

I was petrified. Then she pinched the skin on my upper arm between her thumb and index finger and twisted so violently that I winced.

'What happened, Ma?' my husband peeped at the barn door.

'A worthless wife you have got yourself, I'm afraid,' said Bhagwani Devi.

'She can't do something as simple as milking a cow.'

'She hasn't done this before, I guess. She would learn,' said my husband.

My eyes were clouded with tears, I couldn't see.

'Oh! So you have already started going against your mother for your wife.'

He didn't say a word more, but my mother-in-law didn't push me further either. I realised my husband had a silent authority that even his mother could not ignore.

The point where she had pinched me hard turned into an ugly blue patch. It hurt badly, but I didn't tell anyone about it. My learning process in the barn continued under the able guidance of Lajjo and Gulabi and my mother-in-law decided to be my teacher only when my husband left home.

So, if I couldn't knead the dough, a slap became the most normal thing. To my chagrin, the *roti*s refused to become circles under my roller pin and the number of blue bruises on my body kept increasing. Finally, the *roti*s took a round shape at the end of a week. I was elated.

'The *maharani* has finally got her *roti's* shape right,' said Maji.

The excitement I had felt at my achievement quickly fizzled out. Then it was my turn to sit in front of the *chulha* and roast the *roti*s. The *ghunghat* had to be in place while I cooked. Drenched in sweat and taking big gulps of air from below my *ghunghat*, I tried to sit there like a statue. I tried to show that I could be the *bahu* they wanted me to be.

Washing clothes at the pond was yet another tedious job but at least I could talk to the women and girls there and that was what I loved. This was something I really looked forward to.

Initially, silence preceded me on my journeys to the pond. It scared me to death that they also knew the truth about me like the girls in Luharu. Then I heard the whispers.

'*Maharani* must be really snooty. Does she even talk?'

I was relieved. They knew nothing about the fateful story that surrounded my birth. They only thought of me as the rich, spoilt girl. That was better.

It took me a few months to break the ice and deal

with the taunts but I made friends with the girls my age. And my mother-in-law didn't know that after the washing was done, I sometimes played *lukka-chuppi* with the girls before I headed home with my maids.

Actually, I often played and the maids did my washing. No one had any qualms about the arrangement. But in a village like Chiriya, an arrangement like this wouldn't stay a secret for long.

I was playing *lukka-chuppi,* hiding behind a tall tree when I heard the booming voice of my mother-in-law, a voice that I had begun to dread.

'*Bahu! Bahu! Vishnu ki bahu.*' She was shouting at the top of her voice. I froze. My feet felt like lead. I had no place to hide. I was too visible behind the tree.

She shouted at me all the way home. As her fury mounted, she slapped me on my back and showered pinches on my nape. The mental agony of that humiliating walk was so much that the impact of the slaps and punches was lost.

It was like a show. The way women had gathered by the road to see me on the day I arrived in the village was the same way they gathered by the pond, in front of their mud huts and by the side of the dirt road, to witness my disgrace.

I wished the road would suddenly open up into a crevice and I could jump into it like Sita Maiya. But nothing of that sort happened. I endured the harsh words and the pushing and jostling all the way home.

It didn't end there, though. She made me stand in the middle of the *aangan* and unleashed her repertoire of words that pushed like needles into my bones. Lajjo was standing next to me and I put my face on her shoulder and started crying.

'Oh my goodness! Now she is touching a low caste woman. What has your father taught you? You will have to walk back to the pond and take a bath now…' she trailed off.

'…and meet those women again who are now laughing at my humiliation,' was my first thought.

And then it happened. The unthinkable happened.

Geeta started shouting, 'Roheeni has peed in her *ghaghra*! Roheeni has peed in her *ghaghara*!'

I looked down. I was standing in a pool of yellow, stinky liquid. I hadn't realised my bladder had expressed my fear.

My husband emerged from a room. I clung on to Lajjo. I didn't care if she was an Ahir.

'You! When did you come home?' said Maji.

I was too disturbed myself to notice the tinge of fear in her voice.

'Geeta, take her to the room,' he said.

'No, no, she will have to go to the pond to take a bath first,' Maji screamed.

'Lajjo bring water from the pond. She will bathe here,' said my husband.

'You are changing the rules for your wife already?' she screamed.

'I will build a toilet for her. She is used to one in her *maika*,' he said.

My mother-in-law's anger had turned into confusion. She looked at her son aghast.

'You mean you will get the untouchables inside the house now to clean up the toilets?'

'Gandhiji said no one is untouchable. There are untouchables who live with him in his Sabarmati Ashram.'

Bhagwani Devi's eyes narrowed into a slit and she looked menacing.

'I don't care about what your stupid Gandhi says. No untouchable will enter my house,' she shouted.

She was screaming so hard, her voice became hoarse.

'For this rich girl you are going against your mother! How can you do that, Vishnu?'

My husband looked distraught.

My mother-in-law clutched her stomach and bent down suddenly. I hadn't moved an inch yet. Lajjo, who was still standing next to me, was about to rush to her and then held herself back.

My husband leapt forward and held his mother whose face had contorted in pain. She was standing in a pool of water. She had peed too? It didn't happen to me alone then?

Lajjo started shouting, 'Her water has broken; someone call Dai Ma.'

I couldn't understand anything. Bhagwani Devi was rushed inside and laid down on a bed.

Dai Ma arrived and said the baby had turned around in the womb and things had got complicated.

I ran into that room with the lavish bed and closed the door. I hid under the bed. My clothes still had the stink of urine. I couldn't take it anymore. The way my mother-in-law was screaming I was sure she would die. I was sure I would have to carry the responsibility of another death all my life. I hoped the bed would crush me to death before that.

I sat there motionless, gripped by a fear that was tearing my heart apart. I don't know when I fell asleep below the bed. Loud banging on the door woke me up.

'Come see the baby!' said an excited Geeta.

'Maji…?' the question just about escaped my lips.

'Come, see her too,' said Geeta.

I had prayed to Vishnu Bhagwan and Laxmi Mata from under the bed to keep Maji alive, no matter what. She could beat me up, scold me, pull my hair; do whatever she wanted but she had to live.

I looked up and thanked Vishnu Bhagwan with folded hands.

But when I went out into the *aangan*, the mood was still sombre. My fear started knocking at my heart again. What was still wrong?

Women had gathered in the *aangan* like they had on the day of *Mooh Dikhai.*

'This house is full of Laxmis now,' someone was giggling.

'The *Laxmi swaroop* bahu got Bhagwani another Laxmi,' came another sarcastic comment.

All eyes were on me now. I felt I had committed some kind of sin.

'It's good Vishnu is leaving for Calcutta. She doesn't deserve him.'

I stood in the darkness trying to fathom everything I had heard just now.

CHAPTER 07

Every time a bullock cart would pass by my Chiriya house, I would run to the door thinking someone had come from Luharu to see me. No one came. In fact, I had heard my in-laws discussing that my father had left for a long pilgrimage to Varanasi just after my wedding.

It was as if they were waiting all their lives for the time when they would be able to wipe out my ill-fated existence from that house. Bauji, Bibi and Babba never wanted to know about my life in my *sasural.* The pomp and grandeur that preceded my lone journey on the bullock cart to Chiriya had an embedded purpose. The expensive embroidered *odhanis* that I carried with me were meant to cloak the reality that they were getting rid of me.

With my husband planning to leave for Calcutta, I felt my abandonment was complete.

This thought troubled me when I lay on my cot at night. Now my husband, the only person who showed an iota of sympathy for me, which I ardently hoped would shape into love, was also leaving to work in a faraway place called Calcutta. From the conversations I heard, I realised it was a place that could only be reached by a long train ride.

Was work in Calcutta also an excuse for Vishnu to move away from me? Was he really unhappy with his wife, as those ladies were discussing in the *aangan* that day? These questions gave me sleepless nights and crescents under my eyes as the day for Vishnu's departure started approaching.

The thought that Bhagwani Devi would be my sole guardian sent chills down my spine. I found the equations in my new home really strange.

My mother-in-law was in charge of the house, of looking after the cows, the kitchen, the children and my father-in-law just came and went using the house to eat and sleep. But for the few hours he was there at home, my mother-in-law was at the receiving end of his temper tantrums. She never once shouted back at him or got into an argument. He shouted; she listened. Wasn't that the job of a wife? She was a good wife.

But this shouting, screaming had a chain reaction. On the days my father-in-law grew too fussy about the *phulkas* and shouted a lot, I knew the very next day my mother-in-law would take it out on me. He shouted at her, she shouted at me.

Thankfully, my husband wasn't a part of this reactive chain. There were times I kept looking at him from the corner of my eye marvelling at his fair skin, sharp nose and his intelligent eyes. When he was buried in his accounts books and I went to serve him *kesari* milk, I would linger in the room a bit longer, hoping to strike up a conversation.

Sometimes I managed, sometimes I didn't. If he was too engrossed, he wouldn't even look up but sometimes he smiled. My heart tumbled inside my rib cage then.

I mustered the courage one day and asked, 'I want to be able to read books like you.'

He looked at me seriously.

'But there's no school for women in Chiriya,' he said.

'You teach me,' I said shyly.

My husband smiled; that bright little smile that lit up his eyes in the dim light of the lantern.

'Let me come back from Calcutta then.'

'When will you be back?'

'I am going to work in a place called Burra bazar in Calcutta. Baniyas are doing good business there. I will gain a lot of experience working there and Calcutta is a really big city. Maybe I will take you there someday.'

My heart did a happy summersault. He was not only sharing his plans with me, he even told me I could go there. Then he wasn't really leaving because of me.

What he said next felt as if a stake had been driven through my heart.

'I would be there for a few years. You take good care

of my parents.'

'Would you visit sometimes?' I managed to say.

'I don't know. Calcutta is very far and it's not possible to travel often.'

I realised my happiness was always fleeting. It was meant to last only a few moments.

I walked out to the *aangan* in the biting cold.

The extreme summer of Chiriya has made way for extreme winter. The *chulha* that drenched me in uneasy sweat only a few months back, has become my solace now. It keeps me warm in the cold as I sit in the *aangan* making *roti*s.

I am amazed at my own deftness when I make those perfect circles with the roller pin in a matter of minutes. Then it goes into the *chulha,* fluffs up and back into my hands feeling warm and soft. I feel pride at my handiwork.

I feel the same when I look at the baby. Especially after I have given her a bath after a long oil massage, combed her mop of curly hair and latched her on my mother-in-law's breasts. She suckles blissfully and I watch with satisfaction.

Since Rani was born, my days are so packed that I don't have a moment to think. In those first few days when the baby was placed on my lap, I would feel so scared of her frail body that I felt she would slip out of my lap and hurt her head. I didn't know how I would handle her wobbly, unsteady head.

With the baby too, my mother-in-law continues her carrot-and-stick policy. It is my responsibility to keep the baby clean, put her to sleep, ensure that I give her to the mother when she is hungry and keep watch on her all the time, but Rani's mother stiffens if she smiles at me, curls her little fingers around mine or I look at her with affection.

Bhagwani Devi quickly breaks the spell and sends me off on an errand.

In a rebuking tone she says, 'Done with the baby? Now go to the shed and feed the cows.'

Or

'Bahu, why are you stuck to the baby all day? You have forgotten you have to go to the well to get water.'

Or

'I am seeing since this baby was born, you have become one lazy girl. Is there no work left in the kitchen?'

Slowly, realisation dawned that I am supposed to care for the baby, but not love her. Once again, I dangle at the edge of yet another strange dilemma. But I have become used to love eluding me by now.

The turbulence called the freedom struggle that has taken the whole country by storm soon adds fire to the already-existing turmoil in our home.

December 1928. A man named Bhagat Singh had killed some British police officer and absconded. They said he was a Jat belonging to the neighbouring Banga village, but in my home my father-in-law and my husband were divided in their loyalty to Bhagat Singh. So every time they sat together, it erupted into an argument that never ended well.

My father-in-law believed that what Bhagat Singh did was right and it was only fear and violence that would make the British leave our country, while my husband believed it was Gandhi's non-violence that would ultimately win.

My brother-in-law Kishan believed that if he could make contact with Bhagat Singh, who was rumoured to be hiding in another village close by, he would be able to join the freedom movement and make his life worthwhile.

My mother-in-law believed that with Calcutta becoming the hotbed of unrest, Vishnu should stay back in Chiriya and send word that he would not join the new job in Burra bazar.

I silently supported my mother-in-law for if I spoke out, I knew it wouldn't matter anyway. I kept praying to Vishnu Bhagwan and Laxmi to grant me yet another wish, to ensure Vishnu Das did not leave Chiriya.

That day my husband came back home early and he looked really upset.

'Ma! Ma!' he shouted.

Maji was breastfeeding Rani. My husband didn't come into the room when she did that. He stood outside and kept calling her agitatedly.

Maji plonked Rani on my lap and rushed out.

'*Beta,* what happened?'

'Ma, Kishan is taking things too far.'

'What has he done?'

'He's joined this group of boys who are rumoured

to be revolutionaries and he's gone to the next village looking for Bhagat Singh.'

Maji covered her mouth with the back of her hand, her eyes widening.

'The police are all over this area looking for Bhagat Singh. Kishan is heading for trouble, I'm telling you. You tell him not to do all this. Violence is never a way to freedom.'

'Let him come home today, you see what I do to him,' said Maji.

'What will you do? What can you do?' asked my father-in-law

No one had noticed Radheshyam Das had walked in through the main door and was standing in the *aangan* now. From where I was sitting with Rani on my lap, I could see the whole scene unfolding. Rani was playing with strands of my hair. Seeing my mother-in-law busy outside, I planted a kiss on Rani's chubby cheeks and drew her closer to me. I didn't miss any opportunity to steal my hidden pleasures. Bibi was right, it was best to keep some things under wraps.

'If he thinks that killing the British would bring us freedom, what is wrong with that?' said Radheshyam Das.

'It is wrong!' shouted my husband.

'You do not understand the gravity of the situation,' he said.

'Now you are going to Calcutta. It's a den of revolutionaries. You will preach your Gandhian values when you come across them?' asked my father-in-law.

'If need be, I would,' said my husband adamantly.

Radheshyam Das mellowed down a bit and touched my husband's shoulders lovingly.

'I believed in Gandhi too when he started the Non-Cooperation Movement. It was 1920, you were small then. I lost so much in business because I didn't trade in foreign goods, but I believed in the cause and I was ready to stand by it, but he called it off just like that, after the violence in Chauri Chaura. It was so disappointing.'

'Then why did you go to see him after my wedding?' asked Vishnu coldly.

'No matter how disheartened I felt, I had to see Gandhi. I couldn't let that opportunity go,' he said honestly.

'So what now? You believe what Kishan is doing is right?'

'There is no right or wrong now.'

'Fine. If the police comes, deal with them. I will be gone anyway.'

I was thinking how the men in this house thought so differently from my father. He always said it was because of the British we were doing business and it was because of World War I that Janak Das became rich. He supplied grains and clothing to the British Army, which were much in demand during the war.

I remembered fondly how once my father had taken me to an army cantonment to get a photograph clicked. I sat on a chair and my father stood behind me. My father had specially brought a gold brooch to pin on my *odhani*. He said the British ladies used those accessories.

The man went behind a black box and pulled a dark cloth on himself and there was a flash. Days later when my father came home with the photo I was so excited to see it that I slept with it for days.

'I send supplies to the British Army. I know many British Army officers. They are not bad people. It's because of them we have beautiful cities, pucca roads and we will have electricity soon,' my father had said on this trip to the cantonment.

So his beliefs were at loggerheads with the beliefs of the men in my new home. I couldn't understand why all men thought so differently.

On a very cold January morning in 1930, I wrapped myself in a bright pink shawl and stood at the green main door with the rest of the family.

I touched his feet. I didn't think Laxmi and Vishnu Bhagwan were ever separated. Why was it happening to me then?

'I'll get you books from Calcutta and will start teaching you when I'm back,' he said.

He climbed a bullock cart that would take him to a railway station, miles away from Chiriya. I couldn't speak. My teeth were chattering in the cold. My palms were clammy due to my nervousness. When I left Luharu I looked forward to my new life. Now the only speck of sunshine in my new life had abandoned me.

I soon realised the despite all her domination and her

arrogance, how helpless and powerless Bhagwani Devi actually was. She could not persuade either of her sons to stay.

Seven days after my husband left, Kishan left home to join the revolutionaries. He left in the middle of the night when the whole family was sleeping. His absence was discovered in the morning with a note he left on the study table.

In her pain and grief, my mother-in-law turned all her attention to me.

CHAPTER 08

Usually, I am so tired from doing all the work all day, I am asleep before my head touches the bed, utterly exhausted. At three years, Rani also sleeps soundly through the night.

I wake up and come to the *aangan*. I have to go to the *naala* behind the house to micturate. Now only my father-in-law sleeps in the *aangan*. Rani and I sleep in one room and Maji and Geeta in the room with the peacock bed. Maji doesn't want to be woken up by Rani when the baby cries.

It's a full-moon night, the breeze is cool. I look up at the floating clouds and think about my husband, far away in Calcutta and wonder if the moon there looks as ethereal as it does here. There had been full-moon nights like this before when I crept into the *aangan* to stare at my sleeping husband's face. In the day time, there was no chance of looking at my husband without being caught by my mother-in-law's hawk-like gaze.

The days are so busy I don't have time to think; it's nights like these that remind me of my husband's absence and his unkempt promises. Three years have passed; I am still illiterate and my dream trip to Calcutta seems as distant as ever.

There are still three cots in the *aangan*, two perpetually empty. On one, my father-in-law sleeps. I glance at the three cots now, only to find all three empty. Where is my father-in-law?

He must have gone to the fields for the same reason I have come to the back door. I find the back door unbolted but to my surprise it does not budge when I push. I push again, this time really hard, it doesn't move an inch. Has my father-in-law bolted it from outside? He could have, I think.

After all, times have changed. From the small, peaceful village that I had stepped into as a bride, Chiriya has suddenly become a place where the police knock on doors at odd hours to check if revolutionaries are hiding in the houses. They harass the women and children and often ask for money and jewellery as 'protection money' against arrest and jail.

The atmosphere in Chiriya has turned really volatile. Even at the pond, women talk only about the *krantikaris* (revolutionaries), the freedom movement, and often ask about Kishan. But I can't answer any of their queries.

Baniyas coming back from Calcutta often bring

news and letters from my husband. He worries about his rented house and his promotions but Kishan? I feel he had stopped existing the night he left the house. I haven't heard Bhagwani Devi and Radheshyam Das mention him even once since then.

I'm sure my father-in-law has bolted the door from outside to ensure that no one has access to the house while he's away in the field. I can access the *naala* through the main door too.

I run to it, because my urgency is growing. The main door too is unbolted from inside and locked from outside. Now what to do?

I go to the wall where the cowdung cakes are wedged to dry. There is a small *naala* there and enough stench to hide mine anyway.

Once my job is done, I start back to my room, but then think I will wait for my father-in-law to come back. It is just out of plain curiosity: I want to know when he'll come back.

There is no particular reason for that, but when I look back I think probably subconsciously something was bothering me, a sixth sense that had got activated.

I sat in the corner of the *aangan* hidden in the shadows away from the dim light of the flickering lantern that stood at a distance in front of the kitchen wall. My eyes went to the cow dung cakes neatly plastered on the wall, my handiwork.

When my mother-in-law's attention turned on me upon my husband's departure to Calcutta, I found myself collecting cow excreta at the cow shade, mixing it with water and straw with my bare hands and fighting the retching sensation in my throat.

It was as if she was waiting for her son to leave so that she could get me involved in this abominable task. I had no option but to learn and excel at this task; otherwise there was a possibility that I would have had to go without food for days. And there was no husband around anymore to intervene. Whether I starved or ate depended on my own capabilities and decisions.

While Geeta wandered around the house playing with my dolls, in my expensive *angia* and *ghaghras*, I toiled in the barn and around the house in the cotton shirt and *ghaghra* that my mother-in-law gave me, saying it was comfortable for a working day. It made me look as plain as a pikestaff. But that came with a sense of achievement for her. She could boast that she had transformed her rich bahu into an unflattering, ordinary, hard-working village woman.

All the work that Lajjo and Gulabi did, I am expected to do. They are Ahir women from economically backward families who had accompanied me as maids and I am Roheeni, daughter of the great Janak Das, the richest businessman of Luharu. But how are we different? I sometimes laugh at my luck.

To tell the truth, they are actually better off than me. Lajjo's husband had come in a bullock cart to take her back because her son was unwell. Gulabi wanted to go with her too because she missed home. What they didn't say was their purpose of staying in my *sasural* was fulfilled. I had learned to do all the work they did and maybe became more adept than them.

What took them an hour takes me half that time. They think I'm smart. What they don't know is I am like the horse who is scared of the owner's whip. In this case, the whip-wielder is my mother-in-law. I, in fact, started running even before the whip was cracked.

My father visited my *sasural* only once. Not to find out how I was doing but to inform us that he had plans to settle down in Muktidham Ashram and leave the Luharu home and business to Vishnu Das. He was disappointed to know that my husband didn't have plans to return from Calcutta anytime soon.

He brought with him gold, clothes and sweets. I would have been happier if he had come with some genuine care and concern for me. I finally understood his job of a dutiful father was done, which was getting me a *sasural*–whether it was good, bad or tormenting, was inconsequential.

He thanked my mother-in-law for looking after me and making me worthy of her home. She in turn showered me with rare praise. The interaction felt like it was scripted from one of those plays that I had watched once in Luharu. They erected a stage in the middle of a field and the audience was seated all around. It was marked by loud music, garish clothes and men acting as women. I never knew that drama could unfold like this in real life as well.

Sitting near the *aangan* with all kinds of thoughts flitting through my mind, I did not realise that it had been quite some time and my father-in-law had not returned. I walked up to my room, checked on Rani once and went back to my vigil in the shadows. I was determined that I would only go to bed after my father-in-law returned.

Then I heard a loud sound. Something like a *pataka* (firecracker) that we burst on Diwali. But it was sharper, louder and reverberated. Then I heard a man's voice, a familiar one. There was a commotion; I could not hear clearly what he was saying, but his voice was louder than the other voices.

I ran to the side of the wall to hear more clearly. I was now sure it was my father-in-law shouting. Should I wake up my mother-in-law or would I be too late reaching him?

I just heard him repeating two words, '*Bachao*! *Bachao*!'

There were some sacks of cowdung cakes kept by the low wall. I quickly dragged one on top of the other. They were heavy, but I had developed strength in the last few years. I stepped on the sacks and jumped over the wall.

I ran through the field to where I could hear my father-in-law screaming for help. I could hear the voices of some more men there. Suddenly I realised I was only in my *kurta* and *ghaghra* and there was no *odhani* I could use to cover my face but there was no question of retracing my steps now.

The moon showed me the way. I had never been in the fields at night; I didn't know it could look so bewitching in the moonlight. In the day, the sun gleaming on the yellow flowers of the mustard crop looked irresistible; it looked just as arresting at night.

I ran through the mustard field, my heart beating in fear and trepidation. What could have happened to my father-in-law? Sweat trickled down my temples.

The thick growth of the mustard crops didn't allow me to move fast, but I found a trail in the field and started running till I came to a clearing. There was a machan on stilts standing in the middle. I could see its straw roof from a distance.

The men of the village took turns at the machan to watch over the fields at night. As I got closer, I could see a man lying in front of the machan ladder. He was lying face down but he was still muttering, '*Manne bachao! Bachao koi manne*!' (Save me. Someone save me.)

Two policemen were standing close to him with rifles in their hand. They were not doing anything to help him.

Without a thought, I ran to my father-in-law and turned him around. I rested his head on my lap. His shirt was soaked in blood. His hands were on a wound from where blood came out like a stream.

'What happened?' I shouted unable to understand how he got wounded.

'He got shot,' said a policeman coldly.

'He had come to meet Kishan. We were waiting for them on the machan.'

'Kishan? He left three years back. How would he meet him?'

I was astounded. I just couldn't understand.

'Isn't she the *bahu*? *Bechari* doesn't know anything.'

I looked at the policemen indignantly.

'Help me take him home,' I screamed. I could feel my father-in-law's life ebbing.

'We are going to do nothing of the sort,' said one policeman.

'Why?' I shouted back.

'We had aimed at Kishan, but the shot hit this man Radheshyam. He helped Kishan escape. He has been helping the revolutionaries for a long time. Grains, money, arms, he was helping with everything. This is what happens if you do something like this,' he said.

My head was in a whirl. What were they talking about?

'And the son he was helping did not even look back once when his father got shot.'

The sarcastic tone was unbearable.

'*Paani*!' said my father-in-law feebly.

Where would I get water? The well was far away. But there was a small pond close by, I remembered. I noticed the upturned *lota* next to him.

Feeding water from a *lota* was unthinkable. It was meant to wash the unclean parts of the body. I took the *lota* and ran with it to the pond.

When I came back the blood had become a cesspool, my father-in-law's eyes were turned to the moon and his body had stiffened. The policemen were still marvelling at their achievement.

CHAPTER 09

It wasn't yet the peak of summer but it was a March evening when the heat felt repressive because of the weight of the grief that had descended on the village.

You could make out it was evening in Chiriya when the smoke from *chulhas* unfurled from every house. In the flickering light of the lanterns, the men sat in the *angaans* smoking their hookahs, waiting for dinner to be served. The children played around and there was a din in every home.

But this evening, there was no smoke, no fire. Dinner was not being prepared in any home; no one was in the mood to eat. A deafening silence ruled. Chiriya was mourning two deaths.

That very morning Bhagat Singh had been hanged and cremated by the Sutlej. The Jat leader of the freedom movement had become the hero of the village after he had courted arrest after throwing bombs inside the Assembly when it was in session. They had killed none, nor had they tried to escape.

You might wonder: how does a twelve-year-old illiterate girl know so much? Even if I had wanted to stay ignorant, I couldn't have, because for the last two years this was the only topic of discussion in our village. I could actually give you a detailed description of the twenty-three-year-old Bhagat Singh without having seen him even once.

The second reason for the grief was more personal. We had lost Radheshyam Das, who was not only an affluent grocer in the village, father of the educated and ambitious Vishnu Das, but he was also someone who believed in Bhagat Singh's cause. He had been supporting the revolutionaries. He was father of Kishan Das who was fighting for the freedom of the country.

To them, Radheshyam Das was no less than a martyr who had fallen to a bullet for the freedom of the country. All the men of the village had gone to the burning ghat by the river to say their last goodbye to the martyr of the village.

I had my own fears to deal with. I didn't know if my jumping over the wall and discovering my father-in-law in that situation would be condemned as extreme audacity on the part of a woman, or would I be lauded for my courage? The fear that I could be blamed for the death gripped me by the throat like a noose although I kept convincing myself that I arrived after the deed was done. I didn't have a role in inciting it, nor did I have a role in preventing it.

When the women gathered in the *angaan* and my mother-in-law started telling them about my actions, I stood in a corner hoping against hope that I would not be held responsible for the death. I would not be called *manhoos* once again.

'She actually jumped over the wall and went to the fields in the middle of the night when she heard him shouting for help,' Maji was saying.

I stood there trying hard to take refuge in my *ghunghat*.

I could hear the 'Aahs!' and 'Oohs!' uttered by the women. I tried to peep through the *ghunghat* to understand if those were meant positively or negatively.

For the first time in my life, I did not notice any malice in Maji's eyes. She acknowledged my actions to be positive no matter how begrudgingly. I heaved a sigh of relief.

I was haunted by the scenes I had witnessed in the last two days. The memory of my father-in-law lying dead in a pool of blood with two policemen laughing over him kept coming back to me again and again. I kept asking myself if I had called the others instead of going there alone, would he have lived?

'What ifs…' kept coming to mind and I kept agonising over it, unable to share my anguish with anyone.

Then I wished I had not witnessed my mother-in-law's transformation into a widow. The breaking of bangles, the removal of all the jewellery and the change from colourful clothes to stark white ones, left me numb. Her robust frame had shrunk in a day. The rosy hue was gone from her high cheekbones.

I brooded, just kept thinking that my father-in-law had gone to heaven but he left behind his wife to live this bland life where her every step had to be measured, every move watched and every moment lived by the rules set down for widows.

I felt becoming a Sati was probably a better option than living this life. From that dominating woman who was always barking orders to people around the house, overnight she transformed into a quiet, sad woman whose cheeks were always drenched.

The only silver lining to this very dark cloud was the return of my husband. As he entered the house through the green door that now looked worn and used, his grief-stricken face looked older and strikingly handsome.

The *angaan* was full of mourners and I was standing in a corner unable to control the tears that come in collective grief. Despite that, the single glance at my husband after three long years sent a tingle down my spine that I had never felt before. My cheeks had become warm and that shiver had ended in a ripple in my stomach. What was that? I felt off balance.

A couple of days later, my father arrived. He requested my husband and mother-in-law to move bag and baggage to Luharu.

'Everything belongs to you,' he said to my mother-in-law.

Under normal circumstances, her lips would have curled up in elation. Wasn't this the reason for which she had married her fair, handsome and educated son to the dark, unattractive, illiterate me? Wasn't this what she wanted, a twenty-room *haveli* for herself and a roaring business for her son?

Widows were not supposed to show any kind of happiness. Her heart could have been doing summersaults but on the outside, she maintained that calm, sad façade.

'There is electricity now in Luharu,' my businessman father enticed her.

'There will be maids and people to work for you,' he added.

That information did not really matter. I was convinced now, she only wanted one maid and that was her bahu.

'A new *anaaj mandi* has come up in Luharu. It is really big and business is good there. You will do very well if you shift to your new house.' This was directed at Vishnu Das.

'Now that I will be gone, you have to take over,' my father said.

So my father's plan to shift to Muktidham Ashram on the outskirts of Luharu was final.

'When do you plan to leave?' asked my husband.

'I have made all arrangements at the Ashram. I can move in there anytime I want to. I will renounce everything as soon as you take over,' said my father.

'Why are you leaving?' my husband asked the question that was on my mind.

'I am tired of this life now. I will go around India on

pilgrimages and worship God. A widower like me doesn't need anything else, I will be an ascetic,' he said.

'In case you need any advice for the business I will be just a few miles away at the Ashram. So don't worry,' he added as an afterthought.

My father left, but I felt he had managed to plant the seeds of our move in Maji and my husband's mind.

'We have to marry off Geeta too. Being a rich businessman in Luharu will help you get a better match for her,' I heard Maji telling my husband.

Life was all about calculations, I finally accepted.

The thirteen-day mourning period was over, the *shradh* ceremony was done and the police kept making rounds of the house hoping Kishan would make an appearance. But he didn't. The police had told me he ran away despite knowing his father was shot. I kept thinking if he felt any kind of remorse for that, or did he treat it as supreme sacrifice for the freedom of the nation?

Everyone spoke about Kishan and Radheshyam Das in exalted terms now, something I felt made my Gandhian husband uncomfortable.

I didn't know exactly what was going on in his mind but I was sure of one thing; a person who believed in non-violence found it hard to accept that his brother and father were in tandem when it came to unleashing violence on the British.

I was putting Rani to sleep that night when Maji came into the room.

'Vishnu might want to discuss our move to Luharu

with you,' she said.

I almost jumped out of my skin. No one had ever discussed anything with me in my twelve years. What had changed suddenly?

'You sleep in that room with him,' she said pointing at the room with the peacock bed.

I kept blinking, unable to fathom what she had just said to me.

'I will sleep with Rani and Geeta here,' she said.

'But...Rani won't sleep without me.'

'She will. I will ensure that. She has to stop sleeping next to you now.'

Did I notice the hint of a smile? I was not sure.

My mother-in-law instructed me to carry a glass of milk for my husband and ensure that I massaged his feet well. I once again pictured Vishnu Bhagwan and Laxmiji in that picture in the mandir.

This was the reunion then.

I put a mat on the floor because I was supposed to stay at his feet. I was nervous.

I did as I was instructed, took a glass of milk for my husband and sat at his feet. He was still in a sombre mood and had hardly spoken to me since his arrival.

Sometimes I felt he was probably angry at me for going out on that fateful night. I was angry at him too for not coming back to check on me even once, in these three years.

'You were very brave,' he said, gesturing me to sit next to him on the bed. Hearing those words, my anger and pain dissipated in seconds.

'Tell me everything that happened that night. Don't miss out a single detail,' he said.

I had never felt so important in my life.

'But do you think if I had called Maji and other neighbours your father would have lived?' I finished tearfully. The thought that had been tormenting me was finally out of my system.

'Unlikely! He had been shot at close range. He had lost a lot of blood. Even if he had been taken to the *Vaid* he wouldn't have lived.'

I felt a big stone had been lifted from my chest.

'But I couldn't even give him water. He died thirsty.'

'You tried your best.'

He looked at me kindly.

'How long do you think this has been going on, my father helping out my brother?'

When he said this, he touched my hand that was resting on the bed. The tingle I had felt earlier came back and tightened my areolas.

I wasn't listening anymore.

He repeated the question.

'I don't know,' I finally said.

My husband became thoughtful.

'The incident is known far and wide now. Everyone is talking about it. The police are keeping a close watch on our house all the time. They are waiting for Kishan.'

'Will he come?' I asked.

'Did he come in these three years?'

'Not to this house.'

'I have news he has escaped to Calcutta.'

'Will you go back to Calcutta?' I asked.

'Not if you don't want me to.'

There was a twinkle in his eyes. I blushed and wished he had asked me the same three years back.

'Will we go to Luharu?'

'I was thinking that could be a good idea. Now that we have been marked as revolutionaries by the police, I feel it's better to shift.'

I could feel his breath on my shoulders. It felt heavenly.

'So is it decided then, we are going to Luharu?'

Was he actually asking for my approval? Or was it just a statement? I nodded in the affirmative.

'Let's sleep, it's late,' he said abruptly.

I got up from the bed and moved towards the mat.

'Won't you sleep on the bed?' he asked, puzzled.

'Laxmi is supposed to be at Vishnu Bhagwan's feet, always', I told him.

'As you wish,' he said.

The lantern was blown off.

My husband was fast asleep in minutes. The very thought that he was right next to me was fulfilling. I hoped Bhagwani Devi wouldn't change her mind about the sleeping arrangement the very next night or nights after that.

I lay on the mat in pitch darkness praying she wouldn't. The tingles and ripples kept me up all night.

CHAPTER 10

I got up from the bed and walked towards the full-length mirror that stood in a corner of the room. In the pink light of breaking dawn, I looked at myself in the mirror. I admired my dishevelled hair, the smeared vermillion on my forehead and the marks that were turning blue on my chest.

I glanced at him, blissfully asleep on the bed. That ripple, a familiar feeling now, turned into a wave in my body as the memories of the night before brought a smile to my lips.

I felt Luharu had given us more privacy since my mother-in-law, who had her room on the ground floor, didn't get a chance to hover around our bedroom door at night. In Chiriya, she pasted her ears to the door to listen to the goings-on in the bedroom.

Once when I had understood she was there, I went

to the door on the pretext of going to the kitchen for water and suddenly opened the door. She had been leaning on the door. Unable to balance herself she fell in the doorway. My insides hurt keeping the laughter from spilling out.

I mustered the most innocent expression.

'Maji, what happened?' I asked with solicitous concern.

She gave me daggers. My husband got up from the bed and fretted if his mother was hurt. He didn't let on if he understood what his mother was up to, and what I was up to.

It was always hard to fathom what was on my husband's mind. His mood changed like the monsoon weather. Sometimes he was in a dark and sombre mood, sometimes his face would light up. The latter was when he spoke about his Calcutta experiences. Sometimes he sulked for days and gave me the silent treatment if I rubbed him the wrong way.

When he came back, he would frequently talk about the Brahmo Samaj Movement in Calcutta; how the women didn't wear a *ghunghat,* went to study in schools and colleges and sat next to men at *Sabha*s and events.

'They are very progressive, you know,' he would say.

I would lie in bed on my stomach, rest my chin between my palms and hear these stories with wide-eyed curiosity.

'They wear silk sarees with the *pallu*s clipped with golden brooches, carry fancy Chinese umbrellas and have their hair tied up in a bun. They discuss politics, talk about Gandhiji and dream of freedom for India. They are so well read.'

'I want to read too,' I sat up on the bed, excited.

'There are no schools here.' His mood had changed instantly.

'You teach me,' I said with undimmed enthusiasm.

'I have no time. You see how busy I am at the *Anaaj Mandi*. It's a lot of work to keep the business running, especially in these hard times.'

The clouds were gathering, I could see.

'And anyway, what will you do if you learn to read and write?'

'I will read your books.'

'Thankfully, you didn't say that you want to be like the women in Calcutta.'

'Why? You don't like them?'

'No, nothing like that. But I never want you to be like them.'

Now he had me completely confused. All this time, I had been thinking he admired those women.

'So I don't get to study then?'

'I never said that.'

'Then you start teaching me from tomorrow.'

'Okay, we'll see. Even you are busy with Geeta's wedding preparations now.'

So that was it. He had averted the topic like always.

There was another topic he avoided now. When we moved back to Luharu, their relatives in Chiriya found it appalling that a person as bright as Vishnu Das opted to become a '*Ghar Jamai*' (son-in-law who stays in his wife's home). His mother was elated that we were moving to such a huge house but that didn't stop her from asking Vishnu often, 'Does it trouble you that you are a *Ghar Jamai* now?'

He initially shunned the question but that didn't stop her drumming home the point that he was a *Ghar Jamai*.

One day he got agitated. 'Isn't this the reason you fixed my match with Roheeni? She is the sole heir to Janak Das' riches. It is obvious his business and home will have to be looked after by me. Why are you behaving that all this has happened suddenly? You had decided long back I will be a Ghar Jamai, didn't you?"

Although it did hurt a little to think that Vishnu had actually married me for my money but at that moment looking at Bhagwani Devi's startled face I wanted to enjoy the moment. I wanted this rare moment to last forever.

I had mixed feelings about coming back to live in my childhood home. It did remind me of the loneliness I experienced as a child but I was more than happy to leave behind my unpleasant memories of Chiriya. I felt contented that I was now with my own family, no matter how dysfunctional it was. I had left my *maika* in six bullock carts and came back with as many because we had sparse belongings. This time I was not alone.

The timing of such a move seemed propitious too. Now that I was back in my own territory, perhaps I could try to wriggle out of the clutches of my mother-in-law. On the very first day, my ambitions collapsed. My mother-in-law took over like she was the one returning to her old home and I was the new entrant. She moved from one room to another with a sense of familiarity like she had lived in the house in another birth.

After our shift to Luharu, I didn't really have time to settle down because Geeta's marriage had been arranged. Geeta's wedding wasn't to be as glitzy as mine because her brother felt that keeping in mind the situation in the country, we should practice austerity. If he had his way, he would have made all of us wear *khadi* for the wedding but Geeta's tears did the trick. He relented to buying some expensive clothes and jewellery.

Geeta's wedding had something that was missing in mine. The strings of lights that hung like garlands from every tree, every wall, every pillar, created an ethereal ambience. And the guests and the *baraatis* just marvelled at this play of electricity.

When I was a child, two rooms in Luharu had *punkhas* (fans) which were hand-pulled by a servant who sat outside the room. In Chiriya, everyone carried a hand fan made of coconut or palm leaves. It was a sight to see the ladies sitting in the *aangan* chatting and fanning themselves. The heat was so unbearable that the *aangan* was often smeared with mud or cowdung to cool it. But in both my homes there was no fan at night. The men had the privilege of sleeping in the *aangan*; the women had to get used to sleeping inside the hot rooms.

I remember the day I moved back to Luharu, I had

run from one room to another with Rani in tow, pressing the buttons on the wall that made the lights go on.

'*Bhabhi bijli! Bijli!* (electricity)' Rani said dancing around me.

My father had specially imported fans from the US to be installed in two bedrooms, needless to say, those belonged to his son-in-law and my mother-in-law.

'This is how the breeze feels in the mountains,' Rani screamed as the blades rotated at high speed, creating an invisible dark halo in the ceiling.

She reminded me of my eight-year-old self when I had left this house. It was amazing how Chiriya had changed me. I did see spurts of that little girl when I sprang around in excitement with Rani while we played hide-and-seek. Otherwise, I looked at myself as a survivor of Bhagwani Devi's prison.

But had the tables finally turned? Now that I was back in my own home, could things become different?

In five years of marriage, I had become used to the fact that everything I owned belonged to Geeta. Sometimes she tricked me, sometimes she manipulated me and sometimes she just demanded but I could never say I wouldn't give anything to her that I held dear.

I wouldn't say that I didn't have the urge to physically fight with her and pull her hair hard and make her scream, like the girls did by the pond in Chiriya, but I was too scared of my mother-in-law to get into a scuffle like that.

Maybe the return to Luharu had changed me. Somewhere in the back of my mind, I felt that they were in my territory now and I could have a say. And Bibi's support and presence had emboldened me to do things that I wouldn't have done otherwise. I finally felt I had someone with me who could help me pre-empt my mother-in-law's conniving moves.

Bhagwani Devi took an instant dislike to Bibi solely because of her religion. Then when she came to know it was Bibi who had held me from the day I was born, it became like a battle to lay claim on my allegiance. Strangely, Bibi, who had not seen me for five years, hated my transformation into the *bahu*-maid. Although she had always told me that my mother-in-law would teach me everything, now that she had done so, Bibi wanted me to unlearn everything I had been taught.

She kept telling me, 'Your mother-in-law is getting this good life because of you. It should be the other way round. She should dance to your tune.'

At night, I would dream I am dressed up like a queen and my mother-in-law is serving me food. I would wake up in a cold sweat, the memories of those beatings, heckling, humiliation and starvation fresh in my mind.

Bibi's words, my dreams, my dishonour, finally convinced me that it was time I threw my weight around. Let me tell you what happened when I tried to do so.

Some of my late mother's jewellery was kept in an ornate wooden box locked in a chest in my father's room. Two days before the wedding, Bhagwani Devi and Geeta wanted to see that jewellery. I brought out the box for them, but in my mind, I had decided I wouldn't hand over any piece to Geeta, if she wanted it.

It was my mother's jewellery and it belonged to me. Since Vishnu Das' return, the instant slaps and withdrawal of food had stopped but the mother-daughter duo schemed to put me in such a spot that I often found myself on the wrong side of my husband's passive aggression.

As usual, I failed to understand this was one such scheme and I walked into the trap like a mouse lured by cheese. Even as the admiring and holding of all the gold jewellery was over, Geeta wanted a pair of *jhumkas* (dangling earrings) and *mala* (necklace) from the box.

'This is my mother's jewellery which she left for me,' I said politely, hoping they would get the hint.

'You have so much gold, can't you give me this?' Geeta pleaded.

'Your brother has made a lot of gold jewellery for your wedding. I think you can leave out my mother's *jhumkas*,' I said coldly.

Both Maji and Geeta looked at me as if I was a stranger. They couldn't believe it was me who had spoken those words.

Geeta got down to the second step of the plan. She started bawling at the top of her voice and my mother-in-law started shouting at me, accusing me of being selfish. It was late evening, Vishnu Das was at home and obviously the din brought him to the room.

'Geeta wants these *jhumkas* and *Bahu* won't give.' My mother-in-law enlightened my husband.

He stood there quietly for some time. I kept hoping he would support me.

'Give it to her,' he commanded, after a few seconds.

I clutched the box but didn't have the guts to say no to his face.

'Do you know women who have nothing but a few pieces of gold are giving it all to Gandhiji? You have so much and you can't give your sister-in-law two pieces of jewellery?'

Bhagwani Devi came forward and snatched away the box from me. I couldn't tell my husband that the jewellery had some sentimental value to me. I felt like telling him, to Gandhiji I would have definitely given my gold but not to Geeta.

I watched silently as the *jhumkas* and *mala* were extricated. I heard my mother-in-law mumbling that I was trying to hold on to jewellery that belonged to my mother, whom I had never even seen.

Then the empty box was tossed back on the bed. My first attempt at putting my foot down went against me. Bibi told me the next day that I should have simply told them the keys of the chest were with Janak Das, who was on a pilgrimage.

'Can you ever extract ghee from a bottle with a straight finger? You always have to curve it. Being straightforward with these people will take you nowhere.'

My own wedding day was a breeze compared to Geeta's because I had to fast since morning and run around the house making the arrangements too. I don't know why I felt I could throw up anytime. I felt terribly queasy but still I managed to perform every single task expected from me.

I was supposed to do the *Kanyadan* (giving away of the bride) with Vishnu Das since my mother-in-law was a widow. Like Bibi stayed away from my wedding rituals, my mother-in-law had to do the same at Geeta's wedding.

'End of the day, all women suffer the same indignities,' laughed Bibi in sadistic glee.

'Caste, religion, money, nothing makes a difference to a woman's life, Roheeni. Do you realise that?'

I looked at her and smiled. When I was eight years old and she said things like that, I would just nod without comprehension. Now I understood the meaning of every single word she uttered.

I was every woman now.

At the time of *Kanyadan*, my husband did the unthinkable. I don't know if he had planned this beforehand or it was a spur-of-the-moment decision. But this once again proved how little I knew about what was going on in my husband's head.

He fetched my mother-in-law from the upstairs room and brought her to the *mandap*.

A hush descended on the *mandap* and everyone looked at my mother-in-law like they had just spotted a ghost. The *dhol* stopped, the food remained suspended between the hand and the mouth, the children stopped running around, unable to understand what happened suddenly. I could see from the corner of my eye the groom's father's eyes had popped out.

My husband stood with folded arms in front of the groom's father.

'I know my mother is a widow and she is not supposed to be here, but Gandhiji says we will have to do away with these superstitions. A mother will always wish well for her daughter and it is not her fault that she lost her husband. Then why can't she see her daughter getting married?'

The father-in-law was as unsure as everyone else around him. He blinked, he looked away; he admired his own shoes.

The murmurs started and finally the groom's father said, 'Why not? Why not?'

Maji sat by the side of the *mandap* and watched us do the *Kanyadan*. People went back to doing what they were doing, but the pauses lingered and voices dropped to whispers. What my husband had done was bold and progressive, I admired him for that but he had no clue what the impact of his deed would be on his sister.

I was sure he paved the way for the taunts she would have to face all her life.

'This is all because your widowed mother came to the wedding *mandap*,' I could visualise Geeta's mother-in-law telling her now and then.

The very thought gave me a strange happiness. They would call her *manhoos* too. My hatred for Geeta was as intense as my love was for Rani.

My reverie was broken by a voice. It was a man's voice

and it was addressing my husband. 'I never believed you had the guts to bring a widow to a wedding *mandap*.'

The man was standing right next to us. He was bearded, wore a *pagri* and was almost as tall as my husband.

My husband's face looked like it was carved in stone. Why did I feel I had seen this man somewhere before?

CHAPTER

11

I looked at the big lock hanging from one of the second floor bedrooms. I had put my ear to the door a couple of times out of curiosity. I was always greeted with pindrop silence.

Two days had passed. The house was back to its normal state. The *baraat* had left, the strings of lights had been pulled down and my mother-in-law was back on the charpoy in the *aangan* regaling all women in the neighbourhood with her endless stories.

Since we had shifted to Luharu, she had become like a leader, who held meetings with her subordinates. They came to her with their problems. She solved them.

'The baby is not drinking enough milk…'

'The cow has become old, should I sell it?'

'What is the *nuskha* (home remedy) for cough and cold?'

'How can I make my son like Vishnu Das?'

The last question was asked often because for the women in Luharu, Vishnu Das was the kind of son they all wanted. He was not only educated; he had handled the business of his father-in-law with a deftness that was rarely seen in men at such a young age.

He doted on his mother and was liberal enough to allow the women not to wear *ghunghat* inside the house anymore. He believed in education, so he was building a primary school in the neighbourhood.

But there was one thing they didn't know about him. He did not believe that his wife should also be educated.

I, however, did not let his belief destroy my quest for an education. I had started utilising my trips to the mandir to sit down and learn the alphabets and scriptures from Babba, the priest who was my guiding light when I was a child. I really looked forward to my study sessions with him.

This was another secret I shared only with Bibi and wished to unveil to my husband when I was finally ready.

But my secret was not as dangerous as the one that we were holding behind that locked door now. I felt a strange sense of camaraderie with my husband because he had entrusted me with this secret.

The plate I was carrying with me was hidden in the *pallu* of my saree. I balanced it with one hand and pushed the key into the lock with the other. I slid into the room.

The man in the beard was sitting up on the bed, alert. I went to the table and placed the plate on it.

Kishan's appearance at Geeta's wedding hadn't shocked my husband as much as it had shocked me. Vishnu Das had been prepared for his brother's homecoming.

He hadn't wasted a single moment in any kind of conversation with Kishan; he just asked him to follow him to this room, got him food and water and locked the door.

That night when we retired to bed, my husband told me just one thing:

'Ma doesn't need to know he is here. She would want him to stay but I don't want that drama. If he stays, we are all in danger; he has to go.'

It had been two days since then and this was the first opportunity I was getting to have a conversation with him. I was determined to ask him the hundreds of questions swirling in my mind.

Kishan looked older to Vishnu Das now. His eyes were sunken, the beard covered the hollow cheeks well. The *kurta* he was wearing drooped from his thin shoulders.

When I got married, Kishan would spend hours at the neighbourhood *akhara* practicing wrestling and when he came home, devour 3-4 glasses of milk and 10-15 *chapati*s at one go. I used to laugh under my *ghunghat* when my mother-in-law fretted that her younger son was not eating enough.

While Vishnu Das was tall and lithe, Kishan was robust, muscular and had inherited Maji's fair complexion and pink cheeks. In the one year he was there after my marriage, I had only seen him come home to eat and sleep and I don't ever recall having a conversation with him.

This was actually going to be the first.

Before I could say anything, Kishan opened the conversation.

'My brother is worried about me?'

I nodded. I didn't have the heart to tell him he was more worried about us.

'If the police come, they won't be able to catch me. It's all in here,' he pointed at his ring on the right hand.

I looked at it questioningly.

'One bite and I will be gone. It's a poison called potassium cyanide. From where I am coming now, our leader took her life with this. We all carry it with us all thc time.'

His nonchalance made me feel he was talking about a *mithai* he just carried back from Calcutta.

But my attention hung on two words 'leader' and 'her'.

'Your leader is a woman?'

'Yes, her name is Pritilata Waddedar.'

'She is in Calcutta?'

'No, Chittagong.'

Kishan understood from my expression I had no clue about Chittagong (now Chattogram in Bangladesh).

'When I left Chiriya, I took the train to Calcutta and then I joined the movement there. Some revolutionaries from Calcutta were sent to join a revolutionary leader called Surya Sen in Chittagong, a place in Bengal, but it is far from Calcutta. I trained with them for months because we were planning to raid an armoury there. But days before the raid, the police caught me and I was put in jail.'

My eyes widened. 'Jail?'

'Yes, they tortured me for days. Took out my nails, broke my leg…'

Kishan trailed off because I was looking frantically at the black spots in his fingers where nails used to grow, then my eyes darted to his foot. I had noticed his limp when he went up the stairs on Geeta's wedding night. He did it with some effort.

'But when I did not utter a word about Surya Sen or Masterda, as we all called him, they finally let me go.'

Since that fateful night when he had run away and I had found my father-in-law in a pool of blood, I had nursed a kind of hatred towards him. I believed he had run away despite knowing that his father was dying.

But now hearing his story, I didn't know if I had judged him right. Confusion ravaged my mind. I felt he was fighting to free this country just like Gandhiji. Only their ways were different.

'The police let me go because they hoped I would lead them to my group. But I knew their ruse and I stayed in the jungle for months till I threw them off my trail.'

I was listening in rapt attention. The food had gone completely cold.

'Won't you eat?'

Kishan got up from the bed and pulled the chair

close. He tore the chapatti.

'When I went back, they had already raided the armoury and escaped. They were followed by the police and a fierce battle took place where only a handful of revolutionaries had killed almost a hundred soldiers from the British troops. Some revolutionaries died and the rest, including Masterda, escaped.'

'You found them?' I asked.

'Yes. The Chittagong Armoury Raid happened in 1930 and within two years we were back on track. This time I was very much with them when they planned to attack the Pahartali European Club. Did you know they had a signboard that said: Dogs and Indians Not Allowed?'

'Really?'

'Yes, so you know why we need to make these scoundrels leave. They have taken over our country and calling us dogs. Unbearable!'

Kishan suddenly started rubbing the back of his neck and fiddling with the collar of his kurta like he was feeling very hot.

'Can you open the windows?' he asked me.

I looked at him, unsure. My husband had asked me to ensure no one knew he was in the house. The *jharoka*s in the room overlooked the mohalla behind the house. Opening the window would be risky.

I stood there, not saying anything.

'Oh! I get it; you can't open the windows.'

Kishan slumped back on the chair looking defeated.

'I just wanted to see Ma and leave,' he said.

'Isn't the police after you?' I asked.

'After we torched the Pahartali European Club, we lost our leader Pritilata. When she was shot, she swallowed the cyanide so the British wouldn't get her. I still don't know how many British people we managed to kill. But I have been on the run for two months now. I have stayed in jungles, in villages, in people's homes. I have walked for miles. Then I came to know you have moved here, so I came here. I am very tired. I hoped I could stay for some time.'

So far, I was feeling very important that Kishan was sharing his story with me, but now it dawned on me that he had a purpose for doing that. He wanted me to convince his adamant brother to let him stay on in the house. He was looking for a safe haven.

My jaws stiffened and the words just tumbled out of my mouth.

'What happened that night? Did you know your father was shot?'

Kishan's eyes looked vacant but I felt he was framing an answer in his head.

'He had come to meet me to give me money. We needed to buy guns,' he finally said.

'You knew he was shot, right?'

'I didn't know the police had tailed me. They suddenly emerged from the mustard fields. Both of us started running. I was fast, but Bauji wasn't. I was already inside the forest when I heard the shot and Bauji fell.'

'But you didn't come back...'

'If I had come back, they would have killed me. Bauji would have wanted me to continue the revolution...'

I didn't know what to think. What was more important: your own father or your motherland?

'I heard what you did and I am grateful to you for that,' he said.

There was a soft knock on the door. We looked at each other startled. Kishan got up from the chair at lightning speed and crawled under the bed coiled like a cobra ready to strike. That's when I knew he was carrying a gun.

I opened the door.

Vishnu Das walked in and quickly closed the door behind him.

'You have to go now. The police are everywhere. The talk is of a revolutionary who has come to Luharu, but they don't know yet to which house. Before they find out, you have to go.'

'But I wanted to meet Ma. Maybe I will never get to see her again.'

Kishan had hoped his words would soften my husband's heart but it had no impact.

'She doesn't need to see you. You have done enough harm to her. You have made her a widow.'

Kishan looked terribly hurt.

'I...I...how can you say this?'

'Listen, I don't want to get into this now. You leave,' my husband said coldly.

'Fine. But *Bhabhi* will have to drop me to the station,' he looked at me.

Now, why was that?

'If I leave alone they will catch me, but if *Bhabhi* comes along with me and we look like a couple, they won't know. If you want me to leave, *Bhabhi* will have to come with me.'

I think it was Kishan's way of throwing a curveball at Vishnu Das. He was sure he wouldn't push his wife into such danger and he would get to stay on in Luharu.

My husband was quiet for a few minutes. He bit his upper lip; I knew he was thinking.

'Roheeni, will you manage?' he finally asked me.

Any other girl in my place would have felt unsure, nervous and even scared but I discovered that the very proposition thrilled me.

I wasn't surprised either that he decided to go along with the plan. He so ardently wanted non-violence to rule over violence that he was willing to give me a central role in the scheme to get rid of his brother.

I nodded vigorously in the affirmative.

The sun was setting and the November air enveloped me in its chill. I wrapped a shawl over my thick *khadi* saree and the *pallu* was drawn over my head, my face well hidden. We left home at a time when Maji was in her room, probably napping. Kishan had pleaded with Vishnu Das a couple of more times to grant his wish of seeing his mother, but he had not relented.

Kishan and I stepped into the thin lane as dusk

settled on the haphazard row of one-storey houses in the lane. Ours was the only two-storey house in the vicinity, the rest were all one-storey houses erected without a plan. The lane zigzagged to the main road for almost a mile.

Dirty water gushed through the open drains on both sides as pigs thronged the *gulley*. We walked in silence. Kishan had made his thick beard look respectable with the help of a razor. Three days of eating in our house had brought back the glow to his cheeks.

We reached the *tonga* stand and hired one. The *tongawalla* gave us a quizzical look. In the *mohalla*, everyone knew everyone and he didn't recognise Kishan. I was in my *ghunghat*, so he didn't make much effort to recognise me.

The ride to the station wasn't too long. We proceeded in silence. But this was my first *tonga* ride and I was excited to experience the din and bustle of the town I lived in. Since we had moved back to Luharu, except for my visits to the mandir, I had hardly gone out.

It felt liberating to be out riding a *tonga,* passing by the *bazaar* and seeing the people thronging it. From the way they were dressed, I realised that most of the women were low caste, like Ahirs. High-caste Baniya women like us, largely stayed within the four walls of their homes.

So in a way, this *tonga* ride felt invigorating, it allowed me a glimpse into a world I hardly got to see. I spotted a shop selling colourful glass bangles and there were women standing all around it, trying out the bangles, chatting, laughing and pulling each other's legs. They were once again low-caste women but they looked they had far more freedom than me.

The ride to the train station was not too long. Kishan looked around carefully before he disembarked the *tonga*. There weren't any policemen in sight.

'Maybe we won.'

It was not a sentimental statement, but was meant to evoke guilt. I felt neither. I was looking forward to my *tonga* ride back home.

Then suddenly from nowhere two policemen appeared. Kishan started walking briskly towards the station gates and I asked the *tongawallah* to take me home.

One policeman started walking equally fast behind Kishan. I couldn't see the other one.

The *tonga* left the main road and entered a meandering *gully*. That's when I spotted the other *tonga*. The other policeman was shadowing me all along and I could see it only when my *tonga* navigated a bend.

My heart was in my mouth. Did they know?

'*Bhai, jaldi chalo*! (Brother, move fast)' I shouted.

Darkness had fallen and the *tonga* had only a flickering lantern fitted in the front. But I could feel the gap between the other *tonga* and mine reducing.

What if they follow me home? What if they came to know who I am? What if they arrest me for helping a revolutionary?

Then it happened. There was a cow standing horizontally, blocking the road completely. Our *tonga* could not proceed any further.

I had to do something because I could hear the other *tonga* approaching. I jumped out.

I landed in an open drain, standing in knee-deep muck. I couldn't care less because the *naala* provided me the hiding place I was looking for.

The policeman asked the *tongawalla* something. From my position I could hear only words like '*krantikaari*', '*khatarnak*'. Then he was gone.

I heaved a sigh of relief, but another fear gripped my heart. How would I get out of the *naala*? It was really deep. I was wet, the khadi saree felt heavy. I tried to pull myself up, but failed.

It was pitch dark. I only had the muck and stink for company. The minutes ticked by and I could hear the pigs grunting nearby. I lost track of time as I stood there. The cold, filthy water made my teeth chatter. I was wet to the bones now.

Then I heard a faint voice, actually a whisper.

'*Baebe, Baebe* (Sister).' Someone was calling.

I raised my head and saw the *tongawallah* a few metres away from me, peering into the *naala* and calling my name. He couldn't figure out where exactly I was hiding in the dark.

I whispered back. '*Bhai! Ooreh* (Bhai, here I am).'

He rushed to where I was standing and extended his hand. I held on to it tightly and he pulled me out.

The next day I was bleeding profusely, the clots and

cramps were excruciatingly painful. Bibi said it was a sign of a miscarriage.

I was stumped. In the run-up to Geeta's wedding I had not even noticed I had missed my periods. I didn't know I was pregnant.

CHAPTER 12

In my short life, I had experienced loneliness, I had experienced desolation and I knew the feeling of extreme angst. I had known torture, torment, humiliation and I knew how shame and disgrace felt. I knew anxiety, I knew fear. But I didn't know how grief felt. I didn't know grief could transcend all these feelings and consume me in a way that I wouldn't be able to crawl out of it after spending endless listless days in my room.

It was the dark red clot, not even a palm-length pulp, with tiny eyes that would stay in my mind forever. But the thought that it was growing inside me once, and was there no more, wracked my body with violent retching, gave me terrible headaches and robbed me of all energy. I could not even get out of bed.

Vishnu Das felt guilty, I know. He couldn't look me in the eye, but he didn't even once show me any kind of tenderness, share my grief or apologise for the rash decision he had made to send me off with his brother.

I know he was aggrieved too. But if he had tenderly touched my fingers like he had done on those days when he came back from Calcutta, I would have known that he, unlike my mother-in-law, didn't blame me.

So, my job was to keep my mouth shut no matter what, be it in Chiriya or in Luharu. It was best to maintain a stoic silence. Because every word uttered by me carried a penalty and I was in no mental state to pay it.

Bibi wasn't by my side either. She wasn't coming over for days on end because Amreen was unwell. The more she invoked the *jinns*, the worse he became. I coaxed and cajoled her to go to the Vaid, but she kept refusing saying a Hindu Vaid wouldn't see a Muslim boy. I told her I could ask my husband to talk to the Vaid.

'Your husband? He will care for my son? He hasn't cared that his own is gone. Has he shown you any kind of concern since you lost the baby? That too how…' said Bibi.

Her words stung me like a porcupine's quills. It promptly added to the anger that had been simmering inside me towards my husband, coupled with the sorrow that clutched my heart and refused to loosen its grip.

The only saving grace was Rani's presence in my life. She had blossomed into a pretty six-year-old who had her mother's fair cheeks and light hair, but a disposition that was in stark contrast to hers. She was a small triumph in my otherwise pallid life. Despite every attempt by my mother-in-law to ensure that I followed her detached style of nurturing, Rani had developed a love and attachment towards me that was indescribable.

Unable to comprehend what had actually happened that had plunged me into such a state, she tried her level best, in her own small way, to cheer me up. When I was lying on the bed with my hair dishevelled and my hollow eyes staring up at the ceiling, she would make a grand entrance.

All her dolls were promptly dragged to my room and permission sought for their marriage. She changed their clothes sitting on my bed and involved me while making their wedding trousseau. She went down to the kitchen to get me the *gund laddoos* that I liked or insisted on brushing and braiding my hair. The love and concern that the adults failed to give me, this little girl showered on me spontaneously.

'Bhabhi come, the doll wants to talk to you, but she says you have to look pretty first,' she would say.

I smiled.

'The doll wants you to comb your hair and wear that *jhumka*.'

I had positioned my head on my right elbow and was lying on my side on the bed. Performing a small task like that involved a huge effort.

'She also wants you to wear that floral printed saree that is Rani's favourite,' said the little girl.

I started laughing.

It was Rani's persistent attention, love and constant

efforts to drag me out of the abyss that finally resulted in my first trip to the kitchen in a month. Even after the shift to Luharu, the kitchen largely remained Maji's domain. I merely followed instructions.

In other households, widows ate a different kind of diet mainly composed of fruits and vegetables, but in our house Vishnu Das made a rule that Maji would eat what the rest of the household ate.

Vishnu Das saved his mother from the plight that widows face because of the customs they had to follow. Once her initial days of grieving her husband's sudden death were over and she understood that she had the support of her son, very quickly Maji went back to being the dominating, manipulative power-hungry woman that she was.

Maji had just finished her session on the charpoy with the ladies; she wasn't at all happy to see me in the kitchen. That meant I was attempting to get back to normalcy, hence taking away her sadistic pleasure of taunting me standing in the doorway of my bedroom.

It was lunch time and Vishnu Das would soon be home. I wanted to serve him while he ate, this was my attempt to wash away the negativity I had been harbouring for him all these days.

He smiled when he saw me in the kitchen. My heart thumped. It's strange how I still waited for a sign from my husband, every iota that might imply attention. Just a smile and here I was jumping with joy. Strange are the ways of love.

Lunch was a simple *moong* dal with some bottle gourd thrown in with *rotis* and freshly made dry fruit *seera*. My husband ate first then Maji, Rani and I ate together. For the last one month, Rani and I had been eating in my room. I loathed the idea of dealing with the taunts while I ate with Maji. But today I felt brave enough to face those barbs.

It was a cold January afternoon and I had wrapped the shawl tightly around me. It was a beautiful Kashmiri shawl that my father had bought on his trip to the Vaishno Devi shrine. His new role was relegated to the occasional gift presenter. He made appearances between his pilgrimages to give us all gifts and felt happy to see a bustling household, as if his mission was accomplished. He had got the right match for his daughter, who not only looked after her but handled the business well and the home too. What else could he want?

He had never asked me what I wanted. No one actually asked me that question ever. For that one month in bed, I had mulled over that question and finally had an answer. I no longer wanted to be just someone who would gulp down grief, humiliation and disgrace for no fault of my own. That one month had changed me and I soon realised that.

'So, Bahu, are you feeling better now?' Maji asked me as I sat next to my husband to serve him lunch.

I knew she wasn't speaking from genuine concern, it had to be a prelude to something. I nodded but my body had stiffened.

'Gandhiji will be released from jail soon. He is planning another movement like the Civil Disobedience Movement,' said my husband.

Was he trying to stand by me?

'Gandhiji is in jail?' I asked.

'Why does he keep going in and out of jail?' asked my mother-in-law.

'Because he is fighting for the country's freedom by non-violent means,' said my husband.

My mother-in-law became thoughtful. Did the word violent and non-violent ring a bell? Was she thinking of Kishan? Did she know that her son always left a trail of death wherever he went?

She quickly bounced back. 'So Bahu, you are fit now?'

What was she driving at?

Then she looked squarely at Vishnu. 'You should start trying again. I need a grandson soon.'

I didn't know a mother could talk so blatantly to her son about procreation.

I could see my husband's ears had turned a dark pink, I guess mine had too.

'You have already been married for a long time. The first baby was a miscarriage. People are already asking if she is really *manhoos* that the baby died. One lady even told me that what if your *bahu* dies like her mother at childbirth, then you will have to bring up the baby and find a new *bahu*. She doesn't even have a sister to ask for in marriage after her.'

She said that with a nonchalance like she was talking about the cows and the calf in our Chiriya cow shed.

I felt anger rising from my pits. Along with that, fear. Till now it had not occurred to me that I could also die at childbirth, like my mother.

I looked at my mother-in-law. I hadn't ever made eye contact with her but today I did. The expression in her eyes indicated I was not looking very pleasantly at her.

'Give Vishnu more *dal*,' she ordered.

She had done it again. She had dodged me.

But I wasn't willing to end the conversation soon.

'Who said that I will die at childbirth, can you please tell me? I will ask Bibi to smash her head,' I said.

My husband looked up stunned.

But Maji wasn't giving up easily.

'I am sure that *Mussalmani* (Muslim woman) knows how to do that. The way they are rioting everywhere. Smashing heads should come easily to her. This is the reason all Hindus are avoiding going near Muslim houses in Luharu.'

I didn't know what to say. She had veered the conversation in a completely different direction.

'Is that really happening? Gandhiji says Hindus and Muslims have to stay close to attain *Poorna Swaraj*. We should never mistreat Muslims.'

'You and your Gandhiji. First get me a grandson and then give me all that talk. She is okay now to have a baby.'

My husband got up from the mat he was sitting on. The *seera* stayed half finished.

'I shouldn't expect illiterate women like you to understand anything,' he said angrily.

Then what he said left me dumbstruck.

'Here is one illiterate woman who fails to understand Gandhiji and here is another one who fails to keep her baby.'

Maji took a hand fan and started using it vigorously on herself, not realising that she was fanning the very cold January air.

That night after dinner, when my husband came to bed with his book, he found me propped up on the pillows with a book open in front of me.

He looked at me surprised.

'Are you holding the book to understand how it feels?' he asked.

Was that sarcasm I felt in his voice? I wasn't going to answer so easily.

'The women in Calcutta always carry a book. I have seen them reading while sitting on hand-drawn rickshaws.'

How interesting…

'In Calcutta, women are studying to be doctors, artists, teachers. They belong to another world.'

That's when I started reading the book aloud. From the corner of my eye, I could see my husband looking at me aghast.

'You can read…?'

The months of lessons with Babba at the mandir had finally been unveiled. I had wanted the experience to be pleasant, but destiny always had different plans for me.

'I just can't believe this. How did you learn?'

'I read up that medical book you have. It says after a miscarriage at least a three-month gap is needed. Your mother is illiterate, she feels one month is good enough, but it is not like that; you can also check.'

I turned to the other side, switched off the light and pretended to be asleep.

In no time, I made it known to my small world that I could read and write. It did make a difference in my life, in the sense that all those women who came to take advice from Maji sometimes called me aside to talk, something they had never done before.

My heart fluffed up in pride. Was this my kind of happiness? My mother-in-law hated this new attention I got and that made it all the more gratifying.

My achievements with my books and pens soon became irrelevant since my womb didn't respond to months of scheduled love-making. I never knew intimacy could feel like such a burden. The touch that sent shivers down my spine only invoked anxiety now. Every night, I kept praying for it to happen once the session finished.

It didn't happen. For years it didn't happen. To my chagrin, Geeta had a boy within a year of her marriage and then in two years another one. After three years of her marriage, I was still struggling with all the herbs the Vaid was giving, I had started believing in Bibi's shaman who brought down the *jinns* and every woman who came to the house tried to surreptitiously pass on a tip on how to conceive a baby.

Then Maji's threats started. She was all ready to get another wife for her son Vishnu Das if this one failed to conceive soon. I had no doubt she would carry out her threats, until Bibi told me that she couldn't do that because I was the one who provided her with a home, riches and her son's business.

'I hope you know that if she doesn't want you to be her daughter-in-law, she will have to leave the house,' said Bibi.

I hugged her for drilling this sense into my head and taking away my fear. But I sat at the mandir every single day and prayed. I was terrified I would be called a *baanj* all my life. Whenever I tried to think of my future, a blankness stared at me.

If I had my way, I would have sewn up my private parts and stopped the blood from coming out at such precise intervals every month. Finally, it did happen and without any efforts with the needle and the thread. It happened naturally.

Soon, I walked around the house with a bloated belly just the way my mother-in-law had done when Rani was born. She had to do a lot of housework then, but I just put my feet up and Bibi pampered me with *ghee, kheer* and endless glasses of *lassi*.

Once I conceived, Vishnu Das' irritability also lessened. He no longer aimed taunts at me and on a couple of occasions even brought me books.

'*Bapu* is soon moving into a village called Sevagram.

He has taken a break from active politics. Once the boy is born, I will take him there to seek his blessings,' said my husband.

I cringed at the word 'boy'.

My baby was born on 15 November 1936. I was in excruciating labour for fourteen hours and the *Dais* were not sure if I would survive. I was determined I wouldn't give my child my fate. I wouldn't die at childbirth. From somewhere, I found the strength to pull through.

Maji and my husband had decided on the name Naveen. But once I had a girl, they showed no interest in giving the baby a name. I retained the essence of the word Naveen and named her Nutan. I believed I would give my girl and myself a 'new' life.

CHAPTER 13

As Nutan sprinted down the steps, her braids danced gleefully. She had a *jhola* slung from her shoulders. Her eyes twinkled in excitement. She had her father's complexion and sharp nose. She loved to attend the classes that were held by Babba at the mandir *angaan*. It gave me immense pride that at five years, she could already write sentences.

I had convinced Babba and some of the ladies in Luharu, who had daughters, to start this informal school for girls in the mandir *angaan*.

Bibi, who was otherwise always encouraging and supportive, somehow thought this was a futile effort on my part.

'In our society, women need survival instincts and not education. You know how to read books but can you fight back? Can you change the way your mother-in-law treats you?' she would keep saying.

I felt I was like Bharat Mata. She had everything; riches, spices, happiness, harmony. Then her own people gave her away to the British. Her spirit was destroyed, her peace taken away, her riches plundered. She bore it silently for centuries. But did she not rise? Wasn't she fighting for her freedom?

'Everything doesn't stay the same always, Bibi. Tables turn,' I would laugh and try to dissipate her anger.

'How would the tables turn? She would keep taunting and you will not give her a fitting reply. Instead, will you sit and read books silently?' she asked, infuriated.

I started giggling, thinking of the scene. My mother-in-law spewing venom while I sat there nonchalantly reading books and behaving as if she didn't exist.

That was not too bad, actually. Gandhiji would probably have been happy if I had done that. By learning to read and write I was defying her, wasn't I? Just the way he was defying the British by courting arrest.

'Ma, where is Bua?' asked Nutan.

'She must be in the kitchen,' I said.

We all knew Rani's weakness for *gund laddoos*. To my mother-in-law's chagrin, she was putting on a bit of weight. According to her, at fourteen, Rani was getting too fat and too educated to find a suitable boy.

But Vishnu Das was in no hurry to get her off his back and he was rather encouraging towards his sister and daughter's endeavours at getting an education, a concern he had not displayed in my case.

In fact, it was with his support that classes could be started in the *mandir angaan*. With Vishnu Das saying 'Yes', the other men of our *mohalla* couldn't say 'No', even though they were rather against the idea of their daughters getting an education.

Rani emerged from the kitchen, her mouth stuffed with *laddoos*.

Nutan and I started laughing, Rani joined us. We were like a team. Bibi was kind of part of it too, but Maji felt left out, I know. Neither was she too keen, because she had vowed she would only talk to my daughter if she had a brother.

She was getting restless that she was unable to go and worship at the *Kul Devi* temple in Chiriya because there was no male heir in our home yet. She kept telling Vishnu Das that their ancestors would remain unappeased if he didn't have a son soon. My husband always looked at the floor sheepishly when Maji brought up this subject.

My second born was also a girl. I almost felt Maji's relief when the *Dai* announced she was still-born. But I was inconsolable. I couldn't accept that my baby was kicking in my womb moments back and wasn't moving at all after she was born. I blamed the *Dai*, I blamed my mother-in-law for her obsession with a boy, I blamed my destiny, I screamed, I cried and then finally I passed out.

My deplorable physical and mental state did not matter to Maji at all. She plotted and planned to get Vishnu Das married again, sometimes talking about it in front of me, sometimes with the ladies who visited her and sometimes she would try to convince my husband behind bolted doors. Instead of fretting about what transpired during their conversations, I preferred to remain stoic and silent.

I gave my all to Rani and Nutan and when Maji said nasty things to me, I shut myself off and transported myself mentally to the world of books. I discovered it was a great coping mechanism.

If I told Bibi how my books were helping this way, she would roll her eyes and throw up her hands as if I had gone mad.

Through my books, I was getting back my sanity for sure but I sometimes wondered if the people in Luharu had gone mad. Hindus and Muslims no longer lived peacefully in this large village that had taken the form of a town.

Simmering tensions between the two communities had reached such a point that people even questioned Bibi's presence in our house; every other day, Maji would tell my husband to ensure she stopped coming. Thankfully, my husband still stuck to Gandhiji's ideals of Hindu-Muslim unity.

We were dealing with another issue, though. If we hadn't changed, Bibi had. And I couldn't blame her for that. She lost Amreen. She had called a Hindu Vaid to help, but he hadn't turned up, giving a flimsy excuse.

'It is because of people like this that Hindus are slaughtered,' she kept telling me through her tears.

'We Muslims had such a rich heritage; we had

everything, they destroyed it all. Now they want to kill all of us.'

Looking at her bloodshot eyes, I didn't have the heart to tell her that not all people were the same. I knew how grief felt. I let her vent.

Although Maji had wanted Bibi to stop coming to our *haveli*, actually the opposite happened. It was once again a small victory for me. I insisted Bibi move in with us after Amreen's demise. She wasn't willing initially, but finally she agreed.

Bibi had been after Nutan and Rani to dress up in time for class but we were going to get late again thanks to Rani's adventures in the kitchen. I looked at the two of them, walking hand in hand with a carefree gait and thought of what awaited them in the future.

Would they too end up milking the cows, making cowdung cakes and spend endless hours in front of the hot *chulha,* faces covered in a *ghunghat*? I shuddered at the thought.

There was a commotion in front of the mandir. A crowd had gathered. Babba stood at the entrance trying to explain something to all.

As we got closer, I realised someone had left the butchered head of a cow at the *mandir* entrance. It was a regular occurrence these days. It was meant to incense the Hindus who worshipped cow, but not many people had noticed that a lot of pigs that crowded the thin lanes of Luharu had also disappeared. They were found regularly at the entrance of the mosque.

Riots followed these acts. Houses were torched and there would be *hartal* (strike) for days. The police and some government officials would land up in Luharu in their expensive cars. The windows of the houses would remain closed, the lanes would be patrolled and we would be asked to stay indoors. Then, with time, everything would slip back to normal till a provocative act triggered the tension again.

The reason for a riot could be something as simple as a remark made in a bustling bazaar or a speech by Muhammad Ali Jinnah carried all the way from Delhi to Luharu through the radio.

The next moment, you would know someone had been stabbed, some house would be looted and set on fire and even the women abducted. It was like we were sitting on the edge of a crater, fearing that any moment we would fall into the lava of the volcano.

Babba stood at the entrance, his face grim. He knew this was a ploy to ensure another riot would start; his jaws had that determination that he wouldn't let that happen.

'It is very obvious someone wants us to fight. They want us to kill each other. But should we walk into the trap?' he was asking the men gathered there.

He was the most respected figure in the *Gam* (village). When Babba said something, people listened.

'I will get this head removed and the blood washed. There is no need to talk about this to anyone. I am getting late for class,' he said with finality.

The group dispersed, making way for us to enter

the temple grounds. Babba had averted an impending calamity, I knew.

As time went by, I realised not everyone thought like Babba or Vishnu Das. Hatred found a congenial home in Luharu.

The Muslim League had been campaigning for a separate Muslim state when the British would transfer power to Indians. The Muslim League and Indian National Congress had come to an agreement about 'separate provinces' for the Muslims but the League withdrew from this agreement and declared Direct Action Day on 16 August 1946.

This meant they would go all-out to form a separate nation. And that direct action meant slaughtering 6,000 people in Calcutta. The drains of the city turned red, charred and maimed bodies became food for vultures. Bustling Calcutta was turned into a ghost town in a day.

It didn't take long for that hate to arrive in Luharu. I was seven months pregnant and didn't know how many fears I would have to deal with in my delicate state. The distant screams of women, the roaring fire of a torched home, kept me awake at night. We had two guards with *lathis* in our house now. The bangle seller now sold swords and daggers and had a very good clientele. But my Gandhian husband did not buy any.

Then there was another fear to deal with. What if this was going to be another girl? Would a still-born be better? A dead girl was better than one alive?

The dark thoughts kept assaulting me. I tried to pull

myself out of the abyss but Maji pushed me back into it.

'She will go for delivery to the *aspataal* (hospital). This house is only producing girls,' she declared.

I knew there was no logic in this but Vishnu Das agreed with her. He probably also didn't want to leave any stone unturned this time though he was affectionate with Nutan. He was far more involved with his daughter than my father had been with me.

But at the end of the day, he could not rise above the yearning to have a male heir. As if nothing else defined him except for his capability to father a son.

There were times I felt that my mother's death gave her respite from this worldly torment of mothering a daughter. I thought maybe if I joined her, I would get the same respite. But then I thought of Nutan and rebuked myself for being such a weakling.

I often thought of my father. I had no idea where he was. He had left Luharu two years back, saying he was heading for Tirupati. Since then, he had not contacted us or the ashram. People said he had died. I didn't believe that. I felt he would suddenly make his appearance one day with a bag full of gifts.

But as the streets of Luharu turned into a battleground for the Hindu-Muslim mobs, I somehow started losing hope of seeing my father again. I wondered if he had got caught in such a *danga* (fight) somewhere and lost his life.

It was two months after Direct Action Day but the tension in Luharu showed no signs of abating. We would look at the streets through slits in the *jharokas*.

Since morning, there were mobs running up and down the lanes with bloodied swords chanting '*Allah hu Akbar*'. Or '*Jai Shri Ram*'.

I wasn't feeling too well when I woke up. I was experiencing mild cramps which became intense by the evening and then I was in labour.

I could hear Vishnu Das trying to convince his mother to bring the *Dais* home, because going out in a situation like that was the worst idea. But she stayed adamant and my husband didn't pursue the matter.

Two *tongas* were called. '*Ram Ram Bhai!*' greeted the *tongawallas*. Vishnu Das was relieved. But he hadn't foreseen what was to follow.

I had quickly packed a few things I would need at the *aspataal*. Rani and Nutan insisted they would come along with me.

I was getting into advanced labour and I needed to get to the hospital quickly. Then the guards opened the front door.

The men walked in stealthily. We had no clue that five men were standing behind that door waiting for an opportunity to barge in. They were so quiet. Even before the guards could reach for their *lathis,* their throats had been slit.

They were standing in the *angaan*, looking like blood-thirsty cannibals. I was screaming not in fear but in pain. Rani and Nutan were holding on to each other and screaming at the top of their voices. Maji had run away to the kitchen. Vishnu Das stood there petrified.

'This man here is rich,' said one man.

'Take whatever is there in the house and then kill them,' he instructed.

Before we could see what was happening, Bibi was standing behind him and had snatched away his sword.

'You know who I am, right? You know Chand Bibi! That girl there is my daughter and if you do anything to her or her family, I will kill you,' she shouted.

'Bibi, go home. Leave this Hindu house. We mean no harm to you,' the man said.

'Harm! You are talking of harm? Which Quran has taught you to kill a pregnant woman? Go back and pray to Allah to forgive you for your sins,' she said.

The men looked perplexed.

'You will have to kill me first. Kill a Muslim to get to a Hindu,' Bibi was screaming.

'Kill me first! Go ahead, kill me first!'

The men looked at each other, unable to decide their next step.

'You want riches? Vishnu Das will give you. Why do you need to kill for that? Let us go today, come back tomorrow. I'm giving you my word he will bathe you in gold.'

Bibi had changed her stance.

'There is nothing in the house. You will get nothing. But if you come back tomorrow, he will keep things ready. Let us go to the hospital now.'

She had convinced them. Their menacing faces had turned greedy.

'Go now!' Bibi pushed one of them. I thought he would retaliate. He didn't.

They left as stealthily as they had walked in.

The *tongawallas* had run away leaving their horse carriages behind. Bibi took the reins of the *tonga* in one hand and held the sword upright with the other. Where did she get so much strength from, I wondered?

The contractions were unbearable now.

My husband drove the other *tonga* with Rani, Nutan and Maji in it. It was not safe to leave anyone in the *haveli*.

I gave birth to twins. The boys were named Azad and Bharat. They were born on 1 October 1946. My husband was so dazed and overwhelmed that he didn't get a chance to be wistful that the boys could have arrived a day later, on his beloved Gandhiji's birthday.

CHAPTER 14

Vishnu Das was so happy after the birth of the twins that he genuinely wanted to keep Bibi's promise. If the men came the next day, he would drench them in gold, he was resolute.

He bought gold and silver coins and kept cash ready. I found it strange that he didn't offer Bibi any kind of reward or even utter a word of gratitude to her. But he was totally engrossed in making arrangements for those men, who had intended to kill us but suddenly changed their mind because of Bibi's spirited intervention.

What was it that guided him at that point? Was it the fear that they would come back and so he wanted to bribe them? Or was it his unimaginable happiness at becoming the father of two boys? Sometimes I failed to understand him. Thankfully he had compensated the families of the two slain *pehredars* as well.

The men didn't turn up. Vishnu Das waited for them but they didn't turn up even after I came back with the boys from the hospital. They didn't turn up for weeks after that.

All of us in the house were so keen to bask in the happiness that had finally knocked on our doors that we quickly washed away the memories of that night just like the bloodstains of the dead guards that had been scrubbed off from the *aangan.*

The ambience of the house changed. Maji was always smiling, not a single taunt escaping her lips. Vishnu Das came home early most of the time to play with the boys. Bibi cared for them with full sincerity.

'*Bhagwanji* made us wait so long because he wanted to send us double happiness,' Maji would tell us often.

My boys got a better welcome to this world than Nutan did. The *Jalwa Pujan* which is performed after a son is born is a more elaborate affair than that for a girl. When Nutan was born I had performed the puja alone. No one was really bothered if I did it right or wrong. There was no question of distributing sweets or inviting people over.

Now it was thirty-five days after the birth of Azad and Bharat; the house was teeming with women in bright printed sarees, singing songs and playing the *dholak*. A feast had been organised and there was jubilation in the air. For a moment we had forgotten the riots, the political upheaval, the difficult times we were living in.

A brother was supposed to bring me gifts but I had no brother. So Pramod Mama's son Ganesh was invited to do the ritual. I hadn't met Pramod Mama and Mami after my wedding. This was actually my first meeting with Ganesh, since he was born after I got married.

Strange are the ways of life. No one cared to find out about me in nineteen years but now that I had sons, they were present as my family to take part in the rituals.

As I filled water in the copper pot from the well that stood in the middle of the *aangan*, I thought of my father. There was still no news of him. Would he have been proud to see me with my sons?

Usually, the ritual took off at the village well from where the women walked back in a procession with the new mother, singing songs for the newborn son. Since I belonged to a privileged home, I did not have to walk the extra mile. I could do the ritual at the well in my *aangan*.

I finally got my *piliya*. A *piliya* is the red-and-yellow *odhani* that is gifted by a brother to a sister for completing her duty of delivering an heir to the family.

I sat in the middle with the twins on my lap. I was surrounded by *bajra*, corn, ghee, *gur*, new utensils–some in copper, some in brass, clothes, gold, toys gifted to the boys and a cradle specially made for them by my husband.

I hoped the *piliya* would camouflage all the pain and humiliation I had faced for so many years for not having a son. I wore it with flair, but all through the ritual I had Nutan close to me. She was my first-born, she was the one who made me a mother. I couldn't let my sons overshadow her existence. That was a promise I made to Laxmi Mata that day.

Suddenly, a faint, distant roar rose up in the air and floated towards the *haveli* like a foreboding shadow. Instantly, the faces of the women changed, the *dholak* stopped, others abandoned the food they were eating. Riots, rampage and violence had become a way of life in Luharu. It was something we had learned to live with but the fear could not be obliterated. It was not humanly possible to be oblivious to its presence. The women left in a hurry.

As time went by, the windows of the houses remained tightly shut, women hardly went out of the house unaccompanied by men and Babba decided to discontinue classes in the *mandir aangan* to ensure the safety of the girls.

Bringing up twins was not an easy job, I realised. If one stopped crying, the other instantly started off. If you changed one's *langoti*, the other had soiled the bed by then. But thankfully, I had help.

Maji doted on the boys. She took on the responsibility of massaging them with oil, leaving them in the sun and giving them a warm bath. Nutan always insisted on feeding Bharat and I fed Azad and it was Bibi who put them to sleep. Rani was always around when I needed some sleep and the babies had to be watched.

In the evening, their Bauji wouldn't let them out of his sight for a moment. With all the attention showered on them, they were happy babies who gurgled and giggled when petted and cradled.

Despite this bliss that had touched my life after so

many years, I felt very unsettled in my heart because of what was happening in my country. As India moved towards freedom, news came that Partition of the country was inevitable. Gandhiji opposed it, Jinnah wanted it and leaders like Jawaharlal Nehru and Vallabhbhai Patel were indecisive.

My mind could not comprehend how a country can be divided. How can people leave their homes and move to another country overnight? I thought it was impossible. The leaders could not in any way choose so much suffering for so many people. Leaving home meant leaving their land, their jobs, their businesses, their houses and their familiar surroundings. Could that really happen?

Vishnu Das was optimistic Gandhiji would make the leaders understand and India would remain undivided but the escalating violence all over India worried him. After that incident on the night Azad and Bharat were born, he decided to fortify our home.

Barbed wire was installed on top of the walls. The wooden door at the entrance was replaced by an iron door with an eyehole that would allow guards to peep outside and see who was at the door before they opened it. We finally bought spears for the guards.

We also made an escape plan in case another attack happened. We wanted to be 'ready in case…' but soon I realised 'being ready' was a misnomer.

On 15 August 1947, the whole of Luharu gathered on their terraces. Caste, class and religion were forgotten as everyone chanted *'Bande Mataram! Bharat Mata ki jai!'*

We all wanted to be a part of this momentous event–India getting its freedom from British oppression at the stroke of midnight.

I thought of Kishan, wondered if he was still alive. I thought of my father-in-law and the sacrifices this family had made for the country's freedom. Tears rolled down Maji's eyes as she witnessed the fireworks illuminating the night sky. She looked so emotional, so vulnerable.

Vishnu Das was holding Bharat and Azad.

'Our children will grow up in free India now,' he said. His voice was hoarse as he fought back the tears.

Nutan and Rani stood close to me and Bibi stood at a distance lost in thought. I guess we all had our separate thoughts, wishes and aspirations in free India.

The ambience all around us was that of Diwali, as children burst crackers on their terraces. People were holding *diyas* and candles in their hands to mark the beginning of our independent existence.

I thought now peace would prevail. I was wrong. So horribly wrong!

A few days after Independence, trucks started arriving in Luharu to take the Muslims to Pakistan. What I had dreaded was happening. Muslims were moving from India to Pakistan and vice versa. Luharu was actually close to where Pakistan is now. From Luharu, it would take a day on a truck to reach this new country ruled by Muslims.

As the trucks started arriving, so did stories of how

trains were arriving from Pakistan with everyone dead inside and how Hindus were torching villages around Luharu, killing their Muslim neighbours.

It seemed a bloodbath had begun. It was far more inhuman, atrocious and frightening than what we had witnessed so far.

Bibi wanted to leave on one of those trucks.

'This is not home anymore,' she told me.

'Maybe, this is my destiny. I will live with my *quam* (community) and die with them.'

I was not sure if Bibi's decision was wise. I had heard the trucks were taking people to camps where there was no food, no water and only thin canvas tents for a roof. How would she survive there?

I tried to dissuade Bibi, but she had already accepted Pakistan as her home. I will never forget the day when Bibi finally left.

I had requested Vishnu Das to let me see her off. The *gully* of our *mohalla* met the main road where the trucks stood. He arranged for two guards to escort us to the main road.

As we approached the trucks, the sheer magnitude of what Partition had done to us suddenly hit me.

The sides of the trucks were high. Men, women, children, old people were standing inside. It was packed to capacity with no space for even a fly.

People jostled inside like sheep, their belongings on one shoulder, their children on the other. The babies were wailing in discomfort. Some of the men were shouting and fighting for space and you could hear the women crying. There was absolute mayhem.

An equal number of people were standing outside, hoping to find space in the overloaded trucks. They were shoving each other as they made their way to the front. Some were climbing up the truck and were thrown out by the people who were already inside.

I couldn't believe these were human beings. I grabbed Bibi's wrist. 'You can't go like this. You will die.'

Bibi's smile was placid. 'I will manage. I am going home.'

'Wouldn't you miss Azad, Bharat and Nutan? Don't go.' I played on her emotions.

She took off her *tabeez* and put it around my neck.

'This will keep you safe,' she said.

I ran my fingers over the *tabeez*, looked at the overflowing truck. I felt terribly insecure.

The guards had been talking to the truck driver.

The driver came down with them.

'*Bibiji,* you sit next to me,' said the driver, as he picked up her small box that had her belongings.

I felt a little better. At least she would have a place to sit on this long journey to the unknown.

Later, I came to know Vishnu Das had given a gold coin to the guards with instructions to give it to the driver.

CHAPTER 15

I should be over the moon. Finally, everything is going right in my life. I should revel in my exalted position of a mother to two boys. But a sense of foreboding begins to engulf me.

I am gripped by another fear, that of losing it all. I keep worrying that my happiness is short-lived. If Bharat sleeps too long, I keep checking his breath. If Azad has a blocked nose from a cold, I worry it will develop into a chronic issue.

I check on them ten times at night fearing they will turn over and die of asphyxiation while asleep. I keep worrying for Bharat-Azad, but I have no clue that it would be another person, whom I love dearly, who would give me the shock of my life.

It is the day of the *Ahoi Ashtami*, which is celebrated eight days before Diwali to pray for the well-being of children. It is a big deal if you are the mother of a son and to make it an even bigger occasion, Vishnu Das and Bhagwani Devi have decided to organise a sumptuous feast.

The year is 1947, the boys have just turned a year old; India is even younger at two months. The country has been divided and Muslim homes have been occupied by Hindus who came from the other side of the border, many of whom had walked for days.

They have no money, food and very little belongings and many of their family members had perished on the long walk. Sporadic riots and violence still continue. Since most Muslims have left Luharu, I keep wondering who is clashing with whom.

The refugees have changed the face of Luharu. Their emaciated children play on the streets, many of the women are found begging for work or for food. They wear shabby clothes and look haggard and hapless.

Their men are everywhere; at the bazaars, at the tea shops, sitting at the *Anaaj Mandi* looking for work.

Bhagwani Devi thinks that by feeding these people, she would be able to thank God for her good fortune. But at that point, she has no clue what she is getting herself into.

The *Ahoi Ashtami* fast is kept for *Ahoi Mata*, who is the other avatar of Parvati. I diligently keep my fast, perform the puja and wear the amulet where beads are added with the number of sons you add to the brood. In the evening, I go to the kitchen to oversee the making of *aloo ki sabji, poori* and *seera* that would be served to the immigrants.

As the sun goes down, a stream of refugees walk into our *angaan*. As one batch is being served, the queue keeps lengthening outside the main door. After serving two-three batches, we realise more flour and *aloo* have to be brought if we have to tackle the hunger of so many.

Food is prepared at a frenetic pace and it seems to finish as soon as it is served. The *angaan* looks like a *mela* ground. On the right side, seating arrangements have been made on the floor and our staff is serving food in huge brass pails. On the left side, wooden benches have been placed for people to sit. The benches are overflowing and people are standing by waiting for the batch to finish. Toddlers are crying, children are playing around and people are looking happy and satiated.

The din feels rewarding. I have taken a break from preparing the *seera* at the kitchen to come up and feed the babies. It is around 9 pm. They have gone off to sleep. I am standing at the balcony with Nutan looking at the proceedings down below.

'Ma, look at *Bua*. She is there,' says Nutan, pointing downwards.

Separate areas have been demarcated for men and women and I can see Rani walking in and out of the kitchen, serving the ladies.

Her marriage has been fixed. The *rishta* had been brought from Maji's side of the family so they are Jats. The family has huge tracts of land in Punjab and are well-off farmers. They are progressive, wanting an educated daughter-in-law and they have no issues if she is a bit older than the usual marriageable age. Rani is nineteen.

I look at the two wings of the house. I think, before Rani's wedding, the house has to be painted; the last time it was done was when I got married. I am still thinking of how I would get the garlands of lights placed on the *chhajja* when I hear Azad crying. I go into the bedroom.

Strange is life. One moment you feel settled, happy and smug and in the next moment, destiny takes up a sharp sword and slices your plans into bits and pieces.

I suddenly hear women screaming in the *aangan*. Nutan runs back from the balcony.

She is hysterical.

'We have to hide,' she screams, picking up Azad, who is fast asleep.

'What happened?' I ask, picking up Bharat without even thinking.

'I saw them. I saw them Ma, they are in that crowd. They have hidden swords under their shawls. They are carrying bottles of gasoline and sprinkling it everywhere.'

'Where is your father?'

'I couldn't see him. We have to hide. They will get to us.'

My daughter sounds so brave. I steady myself and picked up a key from below the mattress.

Subconsciously, had I been waiting for this day?

The commotion downstairs has become loud.

We came out to the *chhajja* holding on to the sleeping

boys. The scene that greeted us haunts me till today. Some people are on fire and they are running while still ablaze. There are men with *talwars*, *laathis* and *kataars* and they are attacking people randomly; the children are also not spared.

The front door is open and everyone is trying to get out of there but the dead bodies keep piling up. I can't see the guards or anyone from my family.

I can hear the men screaming, '*Loot lo saara*!' (Rob everything).

I can feel my legs buckling as I walk across the balcony. I wrack my brains to guess what Bibi would have done. Would she have done what I was about to do now? I hope I am taking the right decision.

There is a staircase at the rear of the house that is rarely used. It leads to the small backyard between the two wings of the *haveli*. The staircase does not end at the ground floor; it goes down a few steps to the basement and ends at a locked door.

Bauji had never allowed me to go there when I was a child. But when I moved back to Luharu, I found out what was behind those doors. It was an underground secret *tehkhana* that Bauji had used sometimes to safeguard the gold and important papers from thieves. It is not used anymore but I had kept the keys with me.

I can hear screams from the *aangan* but this part of the house is still deserted. I unlock the door. Bharat and Azad are still asleep.

It is pitch dark inside. Coal is stored in the room to

be used in *angeethi* and *chulha*. I close the door behind me and grope in the dark to put the keys back in the lock.

I guide Nutan to cross the heaped coal and reach the other door. My fingers reach the wooden door. This one is really heavy, but I give it a hard shove and it opens. There is another flight of stairs to descend.

We come to a small room. It feels damp and dusty.

'Sit on the floor,' I tell Nutan.

I placed Bharat on her lap. He stirs. He is waking up.

It is very quiet. It is cold, but I am sweating profusely. I can feel tears streaming down my cheeks, but I don't cry out loud because that would scare Nutan.

I keep thinking of Vishnu Das and Rani, hoping they have escaped the carnage in some way. I fervently pray to God to keep my family whole.

The boys wake up crying. I know we had two doors between us, but I can't take a chance. I kept breastfeeding them to keep them hydrated, comforted and quiet.

The agonising minutes ticked by. In that dark *tehkhana*, we can faintly hear the mayhem unleashed on our household.

As the hours go by, the room feels stifling. There is no ventilation, the dampness making it more claustrophobic. I can feel Azad and Bharat getting restless.

'Ma, I can't breathe,' Nutan says.

'Hold on a little bit more,' I say.

'I feel someone is throttling me.'

'It will be over soon.'

'I hope Bauji is alive.' Nutan starts crying.

'You will be more exhausted if you cry,' I say coldly.

So is this the end of my happiness? I will be a widow now? Children have a way of sensing reality.

I sit there in the dark, fighting to breathe, fighting the turmoil that ravages my heart.

I don't know how long we are there. When I hear faint gunshots, I presume the police has come. I place Azad and Bharat on the floor and get up. I collapse. Lack of oxygen and constant feeding have made me weak.

Later, Nutan told me that she had taken the key from me and opened the door. She had brought the police with her to fetch us out.

When I come to in the *aangan*, all I see are charred bodies, the *rasoi* and parts of the *baithak* gutted. I drop on my haunches and start crying, presuming one of those bodies is my husband's.

To my relief, he is finally found hiding in the *kotha*. Nutan finds Maji in the *puja ghar* in a daze.

Her hair is dishevelled, her right hand has deep cuts, her saree is torn.

'I couldn't save her. They have taken her,' she cries.

My eyes go to the guard's body sprawled in a corner of the room. The wall is streaked with blood where his head had been smashed.

I throw up.

Happiness has cheated me again.

CHAPTER 16

The blaze of Partition not only engulfed our home, it burnt Luharu in its wake. The whole town looked like a *samshan ghat* with dead bodies lying everywhere. The rioters had come from outside the town—from where, no one knew—they killed, they looted and they abducted the women.

Had I not seen it with my own eyes, I would have never known that human beings could be so violent and malicious. The men looked like they were in a sadistic trance, out to destroy whatever they could lay their hands on.

They were also somebody's son, somebody's husband or father; how could they turn into such ugly monsters?

Days after the carnage, the raped, mutilated bodies of women started appearing in the fields, in the *naalas*, on the highways. Those who were alive were found hiding in the fields, inside mounds of straw or in other people's barns. Some were found in the hospital. Many could not be traced.

A calamity brings out the worst in people. It exposed the selfishness Bhagwani Devi and I were capable of.

When disaster struck, I chose my own children. Rani was like my first born. I had held her when I was nine years old. Shouldn't I have gone back to look for her? Shouldn't I have ensured her safety as well?

I was looking at her from the balcony and weaving dreams around her wedding and the next moment I forgot all about her. She came to my mind only when I was safely down in the *tehkhana.* And what did I do then? I just prayed. I left it all to God who refused to listen this time.

Could I forgive myself? I felt responsible for what happened to Rani. Had I gone back looking for her, could she have been saved?

The nightmares kept returning. She was being ravaged by men who had faces of wolves and then I would see her sinking in a pool of mud.

Maji was devastated too. The deep gash in her hands started healing and she found refuge in prayer. Everyone in our house, including Nutan, who was a complete chatterbox, became silent.

Our clothes, utensils, money, gold, all had been taken. If it had stopped at that, it wouldn't really have mattered. We would have probably recovered.

Rani's absence didn't let us forget for a moment what we had lost. Unable to pacify one another, each of us kept grappling with our own trauma.

Nutan often found me sitting under Rani's reading table, clutching her books, with a vacant look in my eyes. I lost track of how long I sat in her room. Earlier, when the boys cried, my ears were so sharp that I could hear them from the kitchen and rushed upstairs.

Now I could be sitting next to them and not stir when they cried. I completely stopped breast feeding them. They were being fed, bathed and put to sleep by Bhagwani Devi and Nutan now.

The neighbours, who had earlier been coming for Maji's charpoy sessions, now told her that looking for Rani was futile.

'*Wapas aake bhi key karegi?* (What will she do even if she returns?),' they asked.

They convinced her that Rani's return would lead to dealing with more indignity than we were already going through.

'No one would marry her now and she will be a burden on you all her life,' they said.

Bhagwani Devi's grief soon turned into fear of the shame that Rani would bring with her, in case she returned. She started dissuading Vishnu Das, who was making the rounds of hospitals and refugee camps, to look for Rani.

'If Rani comes back, no one will marry Nutan,' she told him at dinner one day.

Even before he could say anything I retorted, 'So we give up looking for one daughter thinking of the other?'

Even a couple of years back, I would have probably

let Vishnu Das speak and not meddled in such a conversation. But I had completely changed after Rani's disappearance.

Guilt, anguish and that experience on the day of the attack had made me fatalistic. I had come to realise destiny would take its own path no matter how hard we tried to wrangle and extract happiness from it.

'If staying unmarried is Nutan's destiny, so be it. It has nothing to do with Rani's return,' I said.

I wouldn't let her decide things anymore. I was resolute she couldn't use her manipulative techniques on me.

'If you are so bothered, then you should have saved her that night. I was the one who fought those men and lost blood; you just went and sat there in the *tehkhana*.'

As usual she had hit me where it hurt most. She hoped this would silence me.

Bhagwani Devi was echoing the sentiments prevailing in Luharu. Many homes had lost their daughters to the violence, but they were not particularly keen to get them back. The families had already lost their dignity when a girl was abducted, getting them back would not restore it in any way. That was what they believed.

I had almost forgotten that women were not considered human beings made of flesh and blood. They were merely son-vending machines and keepers of the family honour. If they did not serve both these purposes, they did not have any use.

The Partition reinforced this reality.

But was I willing to accept this reality?

'I will go looking for Rani if no one does,' I said.

Looking at my steely face, Bhagwani Devi knew I meant every word. Her scheming tactics were not going to work anymore.

When you have your back to the wall and when you are faced with such cruel reality wherein a mother doesn't want to bring her daughter home, support suddenly comes from the unlikeliest of places.

I had always thought Kishan had left a trail of devastation behind but this time, he followed the trail of annihilation of our Luharu home and arrived at our doorstep.

His hair had turned grey, he looked old and haggard and the limp was more pronounced now. He had been held by the British in jail, but after independence he was released, only to realise that he had been jailed in India and when he found his freedom, the territory had turned into Pakistan. He walked for days, crossed the border and had gone to Chiriya first.

'I had no intention of returning to this house,' Kishan said matter-of-factly.

'But our relatives living in our Chiriya home told me about Rani, so I came.'

So did that mean Kishan wanted to look for Rani too? I wondered.

Bhagwani Devi was not only elated with the return of the son she thought she had lost, but now she was the mother of a freedom fighter who was responsible for the country's newly acquired independence. She had a bloated chest, a beaming smile and much to show off.

I don't think Vishnu Das was too happy to see Kishan. But considering the mental state of the people of the household, he showed neither exultation nor antipathy. He met him at lunch and dinner as if Kishan had always lived in our home. Vishnu Das was busy renovating the home and rebuilding his business that had been suffering in the political turmoil. He had his own worries.

He was also deeply aggrieved because his idol Gandhiji had been assassinated, dashing all his hopes that Bapu would be the one to bring peace. Vishnu Das felt disturbed, directionless and bereft of hope that the country would flourish.

Kishan took over the responsibility of looking for Rani like a man possessed. He went from camp to camp, hospital to hospital, morgue to morgue and even travelled from one village to another to look for her. He was determined she would return, a determination that Bhagwani Devi started dreading.

Her euphoria at Kishan's return gradually turned into lukewarm affection. I realised, in her heart of hearts, she wished he had not returned with this single-minded agenda of bringing back his sister. She dreaded the shame and dishonour the return of her daughter would bring to the family. She also realised she was losing the battle. She had failed to convince Kishan or me.

I waited for Kishan to return home every single evening in a way I had never waited for Vishnu Das. For the first time in my life I felt connected to a man whom I had always despised.

CHAPTER 17

Kishan became my window to this new world. A world where freedom had been transacted with the screams of women uprooted from their homes, brutalised, held as slaves, their religion obliterated, their identities wiped out. They were living with the knowledge that they were unwanted by their families.

Both the Indian and Pakistani governments acknowledged that thousands of Hindu, Sikh and Muslim women had gone missing. So they set up 'recovery' camps from where the women who were found could return home.

'Bhabhi, I can't see their plight anymore,' Kishan was crying.

He had just returned from a transit camp in Amritsar. 'In all of them I saw Rani, such young, innocent girls. Do they deserve this? Did I fight for this freedom?'

'Their families are taking them home?' I asked.

'Very few, Bhabhi, very few. There are so many of them, but everyday only one or two return home. What will happen to the rest?'

I didn't have an answer. A year had passed. I could still hear Rani's laughter reverberating around the house. Her smell lingered in her room and there were times when I had this feeling that she was sitting on the bed, reading.

Bhagwani Devi seemed to have heaved a sigh of relief that our search for Rani had so far been futile. She had turned her attention to Kishan and Nutan now.

Kishan made it very clear that he had no intention of getting married.

'I live for my country. I don't want to get tied down, Ma,' he told Bhagwani Devi.

'I am also not the kind of groom a girl would want. A broken leg, all nails pulled out, premature grey hair and a battered body.'

'As if a girl has a choice. We have money and you can get any bride you want.'

'Okay, get me a girl who has a broken leg too and walks with a limp.'

'*Hai Ram*! Why, son? Why would you want to marry a girl with a physical defect?'

'Exactly! You said it.'

Bhagwani Devi looked puzzled.

'You got my point, Ma? If you don't want a girl with a physical defect for your *bahu*, why would anyone want me as their *jamai*?'

'You are a man.'

'I will take you to a transit camp tomorrow, Ma. You will see that because of the way you think, what is the situation of girls in our society.'

Bhagwani Devi recoiled. That was the last place she wanted to visit. She had banished the memory of Rani, she didn't want it to resurface in any way.

But neither was she someone to give up.

'We should get Nutan married. She is twelve already. Keeping young girls at home is not a good idea.'

'Nutan should study,' said Kishan.

'Where? In those missionary schools? Now you want us to lose our religion?'

'I will get a tutor for her.'

'Male or female?'

'Since it's hard to come across an educated woman in these parts, it has to be male.'

'Kishan, you have gone out of your mind. A man would come home and teach my granddaughter. I will never allow that.'

'I will sit with him. I also want to learn. I never went to school. Although I manage to read and write but I want to have a proper education.'

'Uncle and niece will learn together? Isn't that ridiculous?'

Kishan was smiling.

'I think it's a great idea. You can join us if you want.'

Maji's anger was as usual directed at me.

'This woman is eating your head.'

She huffed out of the room.

My mother-in-law had a lopsided way of looking at things, but there was no denying the fact that the details didn't escape her eyes.

Kishan and I bonded because of our shared goal. I wouldn't say shared sorrow, because my sorrow was bigger than his. He hadn't known Rani as intimately as I had. Her arrival had made my harrowing existence in my *sasural* bearable.

For Kishan, she was the sister he hadn't really known or met for years, but she was his flesh and blood and the very thought that she had been wrenched away from her home by a mob troubled him.

As time passed by, I realised I had another thing common with Kishan–our thought process. The thoughts that I had so far kept restricted to my head, now spilled out because I had been emboldened by his support. He had become like the elder brother I never had. I had forgotten the reasons I hated him. He had washed it away with his sympathy and support.

Two more years passed. Kishan kept his search for Rani going. At the same time, he started volunteering at these camps to help repatriate the women stuck there.

'Sometimes their family members turn up. They are filled with so much hope. They hold them tight, they cry and then they give them food and money and leave. They cannot take them home. Who are worse? The men who took them away or the families who are refusing to take them home?'

I had no answers to Kishan's questions. I often cried on my pillow at night wondering if Rani was even alive. Sometimes my husband woke up and pacified me. My only solace was he also wanted Rani to come home. He hadn't turned into stone like Bhagwani Devi.

Five years passed after that fateful day. We still heard news about women going back to their families on either side of the border, so I wasn't willing to give up hope. Since Rani hadn't been found dead, there was still hope that she might be alive.

Azad and Bharat had started going to school and Nutan was doing very well in studies under the aegis of a young tutor. Every evening, without fail, Kishan sat with the tutor to study with his niece.

I found his diligence endearing. He had developed a bond with Nutan too. He would get her books to read and they could discuss at length about widow remarriage as advocated by Ishwar Chandra Vidyasagar or the women in Sarat Chandra's stories. I thought wistfully about how much Rani would have enjoyed these discussions.

Bhagwani Devi would grimace when she heard them talking and she would keep telling Vishnu Das that he should be ready for another debacle in the family. Nutan was getting too educated and sixteen was the right age for marriage.

She kept telling us about possible alliances till one caught my attention. Sunehri Devi belonged to one of the well-known Baniya families in Luharu and she was one of the regulars at Maji's charpoy sessions.

Her son Seth Ram Prasad had moved to Calcutta and had started a textile business in Burra Bazaar. His business was doing really well. His twenty-one-year-old son Narayan was going to London to study law and Sunehri Devi was looking for a bride for her grandson.

'Sunehri likes Nutan very much. She can go to London with him. They don't mind her studying too,' said Maji.

She knew she had got me. The fish had swallowed the bait.

CHAPTER 18

I had never ventured out beyond Luharu and Chiriya. Earlier, I had dreams of seeing the Taj Mahal and wanted to go to Calcutta when my husband was working there. Once he came back, I forgot all about Calcutta.

I now insisted that I wanted to go to Calcutta, because I wanted to see the boy's house and family before we decided to accept the proposal for Nutan. The thought that my daughter could get an opportunity to go abroad was rather enticing, there's no denying that.

'You think they would accept if we tell them that my wife wants to see your house before we decide on the marriage?' said Vishnu Das indignantly.

'We only know Sunehri Devi. Her son and his family never come to Luharu. She says they have a three-storey house in Burra Bazaar. But don't you think you should check where your daughter would go and live or what kind of family they are before we decide?' I asked.

'That is not the norm. We are the girl's side,' said Vishnu Das.

'We have to change the norms,' I said adamantly.

'Okay, I will go on some pretext and check it out,' said my husband.

'No, I want Nutan to go too and see for herself and meet the boy as well. She should also have a say.'

'What's wrong with you, Roheeni? You are taking things too far. If Ma hears this, she will create a lot of problems.'

'Keep it between you and me then,' I said slyly.

'But how do you think all of us can go and land up at their place?'

'Let me think.'

The solution to this problem came magically with a wedding invitation card. Pramod Mama and Mami came to invite us to their younger son's wedding to a girl in Calcutta.

'You know, Barjesh has been working in Calcutta for some time now. We found a match for him there in a Baniya family,' said my Mama, while handing over the card to Vishnu Das.

Had it been any other time, we would have immediately told him it was impossible to go that far as part of the *baraat*, especially at a time when India was still reeling under the aftermath of the Partition. But now, I immediately looked at it as an opportunity to put my plan in place.

Imagine our excitement when we boarded a train for the first time in our lives. Nutan, the boys and I were literally hanging out of the train window to feel the breeze on our faces. As the whistle blew and the train started moving, it took us in a jiffy to another world where you could only see green fields, endless array of trees, ducks swimming in ponds and clouds playing hide-and-seek. The train travelled on bridges over rivers, through villages and towns and the farther it took us away from Luharu, the farther we moved away from the trauma, worries and issues that clouded our existence.

We sat together in the train compartment and played Ludo. For the first time in my life, I saw Vishnu Das and Kishan laughing together.

The bunks on the train were a novelty we couldn't get enough of. I joined the children in climbing up and down the bunks in mad enthusiasm, unable to decide who would spend the night sleeping below and who would settle up there. Our packed lunch of *roti* and *achar* had never tasted so good.

As the train pulled into Howrah Station, we gaped at the enormity of the whole structure. The platforms were brimming with people waiting to catch trains, the coolies carrying goods and vendors selling tea and snacks.

Then I saw them. They were in thousands. They sat around on the platforms with their children in rags, their tattered clothes hanging on clotheslines or providing flimsy partitions.

They were everywhere. Undernourished, underfed,

dirty men, women and children. Some of them came to us begging for alms. The rush of happiness I had felt on the train dimmed the moment I saw these hapless people.

It had been five years since we had got our independence but there were so many people, who were forced to leave home because of Partition, who hadn't yet found a new one.

I started scanning their faces. I kept looking at them intently. Was I hoping to spot a familiar face?

'I will come back and look,' Kishan said. He knew instantly what was on my mind.

'We can buy them some clothes too,' I said.

He nodded. Vishnu Das had marched ahead with the children.

I wondered what would have happened if Luharu had fallen on the other side of the border. I could have been among these people sitting on the platform. What was I feeling—compassionate or fortunate?

We had arrived a few days before the wedding. Vishnu Das did not want to overstay our invitation as *baraati*s, so he arranged accommodation for all of us. He said when he was working in Calcutta, he had walked through the arcade of a very famous hotel many times, but never mustered the courage to walk in. It was filled with British people then and he was not sure if he would be welcome.

Now that he got the opportunity, he wanted to stay in that hotel with his family. He remembered it was called the Grand Hotel.

We took a taxi from Howrah Station to Grand Hotel. Incidentally, it was also my first car ride. I had seen cars in Luharu, mainly owned by the British or government officials but I had never taken a ride in one. We were used to seeing *tongas*, but hand-pulled rickshaws were another novelty for us.

I had always thought our *haveli* was really big, but when I saw the Grand Hotel, I realised what a big building was like. It ran from one end of the road to the other end and its white façade glistened in the sun.

'I never thought I would stay in the Grand Hotel one day,' said Kishan, looking up at the innumerable windows that dotted the frontage of the building.

'This hotel has 500 rooms,' said Vishnu Das.

'It's a weird feeling. Last time I was in Calcutta, I was a revolutionary and my first instinct was always to hide. Now I can walk around without thinking the police would be after me,' said Kishan.

'*Chachaji*, then it was worth fighting for this independence,' said Nutan.

I looked at her and thought how mature she had become.

'It would have been totally worth it if Partition hadn't happened. Now I feel our political leaders have inflicted far more misery on their own countrymen than the British did. Was this what we sacrificed so much for?' asked Kishan.

We had reached the front desk. They handed us our keys. We had booked an interconnected suite and a separate room for Kishan, the gentleman told us. I didn't understand a word of what he meant till I went up to the room.

It was not something I had ever seen even in books. The large windows were covered with beautiful white lace curtains; there were brown comfortable sofas and a very beautiful carpet in the centre.

'This is the sitting room,' said Vishnu Das.

'You mean the *baithak*?' asked six-year-old Azad, unable to contain his excitement.

'Yes. And that's the bedroom you will stay in,' said their father. Both boys rushed to the door and opened it together.

A beautiful bed with a satin bedspread stood in the middle. They rushed to another door next to it. I ran after them thinking it could open into a balcony and could be risky.

Instead, it opened into a bathroom. It was the most beautiful thing I had ever seen. The bathtub in one corner really intrigued me.

'A bathroom inside the room?' asked Bharat.

'Yes. And that thing can become a pond whenever you want,' said Nutan, pointing at the bathtub.

'Now don't give them ideas,' I chided Nutan, laughing.

The suite had two bedrooms. It was decided the children would stay in one and my husband and I would occupy the other one. If there was someone I was not missing on this trip, it was Bhagwani Devi.

She wasn't too keen to travel and we didn't coax her. But I knew the real reason for her avoiding this trip. Vishnu Das might have changed the rules for widows in our home, but it was still very intact in the society. She might not have been too welcome at a wedding and she was sensible enough to know it.

CHAPTER 19

When Seth Ram Prasad and his wife Sharda came to know from Sunehri Devi that we were going to be in Calcutta for a wedding, they invited us to their home, citing it as a great opportunity to talk face-to-face about the proposal. It felt a bit uncanny that they had almost presumed that we had said 'yes' when in reality we had only shown interest.

Vishnu Das bought two silk sarees for Nutan and me from the shop below the Grand Hotel. Next day, we were ready for our expedition.

Nutan looked beautiful in her blue silk saree and I could fathom she was excited about meeting her to-be husband, but she tried hard to act nonchalant.

I had heard about Burra Bazaar from Vishnu Das. But hearing stories and seeing it for real are truly two different things. Luharu also had a busy *Anaaj Mandi* and since the migration happened, it had become rather crowded.

Burra Bazaar was something else. It was a huge area approached by wide roads from all sides. But once you entered the central area, the lanes thinned and became supremely crowded. There were many textile shops in the lanes, but other businesses like selling paper, sweets, snacks, toys, jewellery and almost everything, flourished alongside. It was one of the world's busiest trading spots.

'Maa, see that rickshaw puller is carrying so much load,' said Nutan, pointing at a rickshaw that was loaded with heavy jute bundles.

The rickshaw puller was struggling under the heap of goods.

'Ma, Ma, look what happened?, Nutan was shouting. The rickshaw had toppled on its rear and the puller was up in the air still dangling from the front bar. The sight looked hilarious. The boys were already laughing. I tried hard to maintain a serious face, because I couldn't decide if I should think about the plight of the man or the funny situation he was in.

Then we saw it coming. I thought it was some kind of a small train that kept tinkling a bell as it approached the rickshaw puller, who was still hanging high from the handle right on the train track. I got anxious thinking that train would hit him.

'He's in the way of the tram,' said my husband calmly.

'What will happen now?' I asked wide-eyed.

'The tram will stop. It has a driver. See, he is standing in the front,' he said.

People rushed to the rickshaw and pulled down the rickshaw puller. The tram had slowed, but since the track was cleared now, it moved on.

The people who had gathered asked the man if he was hurt or needed food or water. Their concern was genuine. They put back the jute bags on the rickshaw and two men pushed from the back as the rickshaw puller started pulling it again. I couldn't help but admire Calcutta's throbbing heart. Our taxi left the spot.

'Isn't this the address?' asked Vishnu Das, pointing to a three-storey building with a dark pink façade. A short man with a moustache and a bald pate emerged from the pink building with folded hands as the car stopped in front of it. He introduced himself as Seth Ram Prasad. I hadn't pulled down my *ghunghat* in a long time. But I surprised myself at how quickly I did it now.

We walked up two-three steps to enter through the main door. It had an arch on top of it with floral designs made with colourful glasses. On either side of the main door, there were two raised platforms where lots of flower pots were placed.

The façade of the building had three long balconies on three floors. The doors in the balcony were exactly like the main door with arches and colourful glass designs. I could instantly picture Nutan standing on one of those balconies and looking below at the rickshaws passing by.

Once we entered, we came to an *aangan*. It was a very small one, hardly the size of a room. It lacked the space or the openness of our Luharu home. As I looked up, I was greeted by three floors of balconies going round the *aangan*. The balconies had wrought-iron banisters and wooden *jalis* hung from the top to offer shade from the sun.

We were taken to a room on the ground floor, the *baithak*. It was a large room with brown velvet sofas. There was a wooden centre table and a large chandelier hanging from the ceiling. It not only brightened up the room, it lent it a regal aura. My eyes went to the two wooden cabinets full of books. It was those cabinets that held my fancy. I realised it was the same for my husband.

'Whose books are those?' he asked.

'Those belong to my two sons. My eldest lives in Calcutta and handles our business with me. The second is Narayan, he is studying Law and will be going to London for further studies.' said Ram Prasad.

'Your daughter can go with him to London. She can join a school there. My mother Sunehri Devi was saying she is very good in studies,' he added.

Nutan was sitting demurely on the sofa. My ears propped up the moment he mentioned studying in London.

Sharda Devi entered with her elder daughter-in-law Poorvi. They were carrying plates of food.

'This is a delicacy of Bengal, *luchi* and *floor dom* that we prepared specially for you,' she said. Both she and her daughter-in-law had covered their head with the *pallu* of the saree, but it was not drawn to cover their face. I heaved a sigh of relief.

'*Arrey, Narayan ko bulao*, (Call Narayan)' said Seth Ram Prasad. Nutan had stiffened a bit. She nervously kept looking at the books.

Narayan reminded me of Vishnu Das at his age. He had the same lithe frame, handsome face and twinkling eyes. He was less fair, though. Although hours in the sun at the *Anaaj Mandi* had made my husband tanned, he was still very fair. Was I actually comparing them? I smiled to myself.

I could see Nutan's cheeks turning red as she stole glances at Narayan. Their chemistry was instantaneous. Cupid had struck.

It is a strange feeling to realise that your daughter has grown up and is feeling attracted to a man. I thought about the tinkles and chills I felt seeing my husband as a teenager. Where did those thrills vanish?

I glanced at my husband as if hoping I would feel the same again. But my eyes landed on Azad and Bharat who were precariously toying with a tea cup. I gently pulled them aside and made them sit on the sofa.

I knew Nutan had questions for Narayan, especially after she laid eyes on all those books, but we had still not come to that stage where the bride and groom could talk before marriage. Considering how Vishnu Das and I were married, we had still come a long way.

She was listening intently as her father was asking her to-be husband some questions.

'I want to come back from London and practice in Calcutta,' said Narayan.

'You want to do civil or criminal law?' asked my husband.

'Criminal.'

Nutan shot him an admiring glance. I knew there was no looking back now.

Sharda Devi soon took me inside, because we still were in the age when men and women did not sit together for long and talk, even if it was a wedding they were discussing. But in a way, that was good because I got to know her better and tried hard to fathom if she had a Bhagwani Devi lurking inside her.

Sharda Devi was also short, she had a sweet face and unlike me, she was fair. She came across as docile and soft-spoken. I hoped fervently there wasn't a mother-in-law side to her that was only reserved for Nutan. Years later I realised she should have been the least of my worries.

I got to see two of their bedrooms on the first floor and even used the huge bathroom that was at the end of the balcony. The brass bathtub impressed me immensely.

Although the rooms were large, they lacked a sense of space. Maybe because there was too much furniture packed into each room—large almirahs, huge four poster beds, dressing tables and high chairs. The rooms reeked of wealth, but lacked the lived-in feeling.

Soon I came to realise the *luchi* and *aloor dom* had been served as snacks and a meal was awaiting us in the dining room. We still sat on the floor and ate in Luharu, but here, a large teak wood eight-seater table stood in the middle of an airy room on the ground floor, next to the kitchen. What caught my attention were the five kinds of Bengali sweets, from *pantua, rajbhog, sandesh, kalakand* to *mishti doi*.

For a moment I missed Rani. She was the only one in our family who had a sweet tooth and would have devoured it all by now. I thought about how I had moved on. I was already planning another wedding and had forgotten all about the wedding that never took place. I felt guilty.

Kishan was observant but quiet throughout the proceedings. When we went back to the hotel, he said only one thing.

'I found the father-in-law shifty.'

'Why?' asked my husband.

'He could never look eye-to-eye and talk,' said Kishan.

I wasn't paying much attention to him, maybe because I desperately wanted nothing to go wrong. I wanted my daughter to have the best life ever. Far, far better than the one I had.

Nutan was unpacking the glass bangles that she had bought from a huge store in Burra Bazaar. A set of bangles was wrapped in a pamphlet. She read what was written on it and suddenly became quiet.

I picked up the piece of paper. It was a pamphlet printed by the Ministry of Relief and Rehabilitation urging people to take home the women who were rescued after Partition.

It read: Just as a flowing stream purifies itself and is washed clean of pollutants, so is a menstruating woman purified after her periods.

So, it was not only Bhagwani Devi who did not want

her daughter back; there was a nation full of people out there who too felt the same.

The wound that we had suppressed in our quest for happiness came back hideously raw and inflamed.

CHAPTER 20

'I don't know why but I feel if she is still alive, she would be in India. The miscreants who came that night were from a neighbouring village. The village is empty now, they have all left for Pakistan. Don't you think it would be too risky to take along Hindu abducted women with them across the border?' asked Kishan.

He was packing his bags. He was leaving for Jalandhar. It had the largest women's camp where rescued women were being sheltered, where they could be contacted by their families. Kishan planned to volunteer in that camp and stay on for a few months in case he got news of Rani.

'If she has been converted and married, then she could have been taken across the border. By now we know that so many women have been converted,' I said.

'That's true. I have been going to these camps for almost five years now. It's a strange dichotomy. Now there are women with children who are married to their abductors or protectors and don't want to go to Pakistan. Same is the situation in Pakistan; they don't want to come back but were forced to leave their children and come to India. Even if the women are accepted, their Hindu families would not accept their Muslim children. They are being uprooted for a second time now,' said Kishan.

'Do you think Rani is married to someone, somewhere, has children and has her own home? We are probably worrying unnecessarily,' I asked.

'Could be, but we can't give up the search. At least we need to know she is well and happy,' said my brother-in-law.

With Kishan in Jalandhar, Nutan married and settled in Calcutta six months back, the boys in school and my kitchen duties done by 10 am, I felt lonely. Still, the last person I wanted to have a conversation with was Maji. She had become old, suffered from arthritis, but her nature remained as belligerent as ever.

The house seemed to have gone back to those silent days of my childhood. I missed Bibi sometimes. I hoped she was well and settled in Pakistan. Just a few years back, Bibi and I lived in the same house. Now we belong to two separate countries with such enmity that if you wired a message, you could be considered a spy. A Hindu going to meet a Muslim friend or a Muslim coming to meet a Hindu Indian across the border, was out of question.

I often thought of my father. I was sure he was no more. But I didn't feel as dejected by his absence as I felt about Rani's. He had lived a full life and was living life on his own terms when he disappeared. She was a young girl dreaming of starting a new life when circumstances ruined everything.

If I looked down from the *chhajja*, I could still see her walking hurriedly in and out of the kitchen, serving that huge crowd of people and then...

It was a memory that I had tried to consciously block. Had tried to forget and move on. The impact of some events on your psyche is so deep that no matter how much you want to shut it away, it resurfaces, sometimes at the oddest of moments.

At Nutan's wedding, when she was taking the *phera*s, the sight of the fire brought back visions of the gutted ground floor of the *haveli*, of the charred bodies lying in the *aangan*. The chants of the pundit transformed into screams of the women and children. Then I saw my father-in-law running through a field and jumping into a fire. I sat there frozen, the hallucinations threatening to break down my fragile veneer.

Vishnu Das, who was standing next to me, understood I was having an episode. He offered me a glass of water and talked to me softly, bringing me back to reality. Looking back, I feel I could have collapsed and the mother of the bride fainting at the wedding could have been deduced as something ominous. The superstitions in our community could take new forms any moment. I was glad my husband averted a situation like that.

My only solace was that Nutan was settled now.

Although I missed her constant chatter, I was happy that she was with a man who would take her life forward. She was supposed to leave with him for London soon and I hoped she could go to school there and get a formal education.

Nutan wrote to me often. This was something I looked forward to now. It was a pleasure to read and re-read her letters written in her impeccable handwriting.

But the letter she wrote last month left me a bit confused. Here is what she wrote.

> *Dear Ma,*
>
> *I miss you, Bauji and my brothers dearly. Living in a big city like Calcutta is totally different. Here everything goes at such a fast pace. I wake up at 6 am and make tea and breakfast with Poorvi Didi. We decide on the breakfast menu the night before and get down to work early in the morning.*
>
> *I am usually free by 10 am. Maji wakes up much later. She makes lunch. We have two people to help in the kitchen with the chopping and grinding. Maji is a very sweet person. She does not interfere when we are in the kitchen and doesn't like us hovering around when she is cooking.*
>
> *She feels very happy that I already know cooking, can make excellent tea, keep the house tidy and she tells me I must join a school to take formal education. There is a girls' school in the vicinity and every day I stand in the balcony seeing the girls passing by in blue-bordered white sarees, the school uniform. It*

reminds me of our classes at the mandir aangan and how Bua and I would run with our jholas swinging from our shoulders. We laughed so much when you couldn't keep pace.

I could stand on that balcony all day. The road below is so crowded and there is so much going on all the time. Women are so free here. They go to school, even college, go out shopping and they are rarely accompanied by men.

Sometimes Poorvi Didi and I go out in a rickshaw to do some shopping. I really enjoy buying sarees, bangles and jutis. Maji gives us money to shop and she is really generous. She sometimes comes along with us too.

When she comes, she always takes us to Madras Tiffin, a restaurant near our house. I love their dosa, idli and upma. Ma, South Indian food is so different from our food. When you come next time I will take you there.

*I like Bengali food too. Maji knows a lot of Bengali dishes and cooks them at home. Food is an absolute enjoyment here. Puchka*s *are another thing we have often. There's a puchkawalla who comes to our mohalla every day. All the women come down in the evening to have puchka from him. If you watch from the balcony, it's wonderful to see the women standing in a circle around the puchkawalla in their brightly printed sarees and shoving the puchka*s *in their mouth. You have to have one whole puchka at* *one go. It tastes heavenly.*

But my most exciting experience was our visit to College Street. I didn't know that a place like this could exist. It is a long stretch of road with stalls and stalls of books and a lot of second-hand books also. It is not very far from where we live, so I bought a lot of books and I came back home in a rickshaw.

I could spend one entire day there. Why one day? Many days.

I saw Presidency College. It's so huge and beautiful. So many women study there. I hope I can go to college one day.

Everyone in my sasural is very enthusiastic about my interest in studies except for my father-in-law. He is not the person he pretends to be.

I have heard talk that my husband might be leaving for London alone and I might be joining a school in Calcutta for now. I would join him later.

I will keep you posted about everything in my next letter.

Regards
Nutan

To me, two things came across as odd in this letter. There was no mention of Narayan except for the last line. Also, what did she mean that he would be going alone to London? What happened to all those plans of the two of them going together?

CHAPTER 21

The foundations of the building were laid by Vishnu Das when we had moved to Luharu years back. He had an ambitious plan for starting a school for girls, so he had bought a huge plot of land. Then the situation changed and he had to spend all his time keeping his business together.

He got so busy in his daily struggle that the school remained at the stage of a few pillars with iron rods sticking out from them. The first day I went to the location, I was greeted by a barely-constructed base and cows grazing on the green grass.

Some children were playing *lukka-chuppi* among the pillars. I looked up at the wide blue sky over the plot and it seemed like a dream waiting to happen. I could see a beautiful building taking shape and girls in braids gaily running around in school uniforms.

'What will we name the school?' Vishnu Das asked.

Without a thought I said, 'Rani Devi Balika Vidyalaya.' He looked at me doubtfully. 'Do you think it's a good idea considering people know what happened to Rani?'

'No, they don't know. None of us know,' I said stubbornly.

'But still…'

I glared at my husband.

'How about Nutan Kanya Vidyalaya?' he asked.

'I'll think about it,' I said.

Setting up a school is not an easy task. That's something I realised when I got more and more involved in the whole process. People in Luharu were still tentative about sending their girls to schools. They were worried that if their daughters got too much education, it would be difficult to find a match for them.

Marriage and being the mother of a boy, was still far more important than being educated; India gaining independence had not changed any of that. On top of that, the only schools in the vicinity were Christian missionary schools and people were really wary about sending their girls to study there because they believed these were places that promoted Christian faith.

Earlier, I could get some neighbours to send their girls to Babba's classes in the temple courtyard, but persuading them to try a proper school was not going to be an easy task. I thought of taking Babba's help in convincing people. I had planned that once the building was complete, we would embark on a door-to-door campaign.

But before that, I had to straighten out something more important.

'Have you seen how these Ahir and Jat boys taunt the girls on the streets?' said Bhagwani Devi one day.

'If girls walk down to school, these boys will be after them. Who will take responsibility for them, you?' she taunted me.

Maji and I were like two prisoners in the same jail cell. You get to know each other too well, because you don't have an option but that does not mean you like each other.

I knew she was trying to discourage me from starting the school. But I could not overlook the fact that she had a point.

It's six years since Partition but women are anything but safe in the country. Abductions are still common. Lower caste women being picked up by upper caste men is the norm. What happens to them after that, no one knows. No one really cares.

No FIRs are lodged at the police stations. No one is arrested. Life goes on as usual. I find the whole situation appalling. During Partition, we blamed religious enmity for the disappearance of girls. Now what was happening? Who was to blame?

Women would always be unsafe, I concluded, no matter what the political or social situation.

'Maybe a hostel could be a solution to this problem,' I told Vishnu Das.

The ground floor of our school had been constructed

and we were walking around the corridors and the classrooms to ensure everything was in place. There were five classrooms on the ground floor. Sunlight streamed through the big windows. I could see myself sitting in that room as a thirteen-year-old girl, a dream that I always nursed but that never came true.

'That would be a lot of responsibility,' said my husband.

'That would ensure their safety too,' I said.

Even as I was saying that, I had doubts. We could not ensure safety for one girl in the family and I was promising to keep other girls safe. Maybe I was aiming too high and should stop.

Vishnu Das had expanded his business and started trading in Calcutta. He went to visit Nutan whenever he was there. On his last visit, he brought news that Narayan was leaving for London in a few days and Nutan wasn't going with him. They cited some visa issues and said she would join him later.

'Is she disappointed?' I asked Vishnu Das.

'No, she's fine. In fact, I feel she is not too keen to go to London. I may be wrong,' he said.

'Really? What did she say?'

'She told me that she wanted to come to Luharu and see the school. She seemed keener on that.'

'But they had promised she would be in London,' I said, disappointed, unable to tell my husband that was probably the singular reason I agreed to Nutan's wedding.

'We are from the girl's side; we cannot ask too many

questions. That doesn't look good. Our daughter is theirs now, they will know what's best for her.'

I could have throttled Vishnu Das for saying this. But I controlled my anger. That was the reason no one came to see me for years and left me at the mercy of Bhagwani Devi.

Would I allow the same rules to apply to my daughter?

Six months later, I received a letter from Nutan that read more like an SOS.

> *Dear Ma,*
>
> *Hope all of you are doing well. I am fine too. I haven't been home in a long time. Can you tell Bauji to take me to Luharu next time he is here? Please Ma. Please can you tell him?*
>
> *I am dying to see you all. I miss my brothers.*
>
> *Reply quickly and tell me when Bauji will come. I will be ready then.*
>
> *Regards*
> *Nutan*

Something was wrong, I was sure. Her earlier letters were rambling anecdotes of her life in Calcutta that I loved reading. She had never before written a letter that was short, to the point.

I tried hard to read between the lines and understand what she implied, what she meant. But I could not make head or tail of it.

I didn't send a reply to the letter.

CHAPTER 22

I had never been in a more tranquil setting. I was sitting under a tree. A green expanse stretched in front of me, only to end under a canopy where a group of boys and girls sat in yellow matching dresses. A teacher was walking around teaching them. From where I was sitting, I could not hear what he was saying, but I could see the rapt attention on the faces of his students.

Rabindranath Tagore's Santiniketan had always intrigued me. He started the school in 1901 with five students and now right in front of my eyes I could see the most beautiful thing possible: an outdoor class in progress with around 30 students. Since the time I got involved in building our school, I had wanted to see Santiniketan. I wanted to know how this place functioned with classes held under trees, in a natural environment and how students learned under the *Gurukul* system.

I could see the yellow building of the Patha Bhavana School in the distance. The quaint two-storey building with the red-tiled sun shade on the windows shone in the sunshine. The flame flowers in full bloom on the trees in front of the building made it look like an artist's canvas.

With the building in the backdrop, I saw the familiar silhouette of a girl walking through the red dirt road towards me. I knew that sprightly gait so well.

'Ma, it's so peaceful here. I took a walk around the entire campus,' Nutan said as she came and sat next to me under the tree.

I looked at her serene face. It gave away none of the turmoil that she had been going through. It is really strange how women have an in-built mechanism to accept misfortune, deal with it and still live on like nothing had happened.

I had not replied to Nutan's letter. Instead, I went to Calcutta with Vishnu Das immediately. I had a sense of urgency. I wanted to reach her before the mail could.

Kishan had returned from Jalandhar just then. Needless to say, his search for Rani was still futile. We left Azad and Bharat with him and Maji and took the first train to Calcutta.

We checked in at the Grand Hotel again. It's amazing how experience changes you. This time there was no amazement, no wide-eyed wonder at satin beds and lace curtains. We walked into our rooms like that was a way of life we had always been used to.

Soon we found ourselves in Nutan's *sasural*, in that

sitting room with brown sofas and the glowing chandelier.

But the room looked more sombre now, perhaps because of the people who populated it. That genial smiling face of my daughter's *saas* had taken on a hardened expression. Nutan walked in with tea and samosas. She was smiling but I instinctively felt she was hiding something. It was a mystery that I had to unravel.

'We want to take Nutan home with us to Luharu for a few days,' Vishnu Das was saying.

'Why do you want to take her? Any particular reason?' asked her father-in-law Seth Ram Prasad. He sounded curt.

'Oh! It's nothing in particular. Narayan is not here and she might like to spend some time with her brothers back home,' said my husband.

'*Sambandhiji*, it doesn't matter if Narayan is here or not. For a married woman, her *sasural* is her home. In our home, women don't go to their *maika*,' he said.

He touched the top of Nutan's head with affection as she handed him the cup. 'And we can't do without our *Chhoti Bahu* for a moment. Can we?'

His touch made Nutan recoil as if the slimy skin of a snake touched her body. She immediately reverted to normal but my eyes didn't miss this fleeting aberration.

'Who will help me around the house if she is gone?' asked Sharda Devi.

As far as I could make out from Nutan's letters, they had servants and the elder daughter-in-law Poorvi was also there to help out Sharda Devi.

Why were they so reluctant to let her go? Was there something more to it?

'I'm afraid she can't go. You are welcome to visit us but she can't go,' said Ram Prasad with finality.

Nutan was looking at me pleadingly. I was tongue-tied.

'If you don't want her to go, we won't take her,' said Vishnu Das.

Nutan looked at us wide-eyed. For the first time, I saw fear in those pupils.

'But can we take her with us to Santiniketan for a few days? I know she has always wanted to see Rabindranath Tagore's ashram and it's only a few hours by train from here.'

I thanked God for my husband's presence of mind. I was certain he could also sense something was amiss.

'How many days?' asked the father-in-law.

'Three days maybe,' said my husband.

'All right, not more than three days.'

'So can she come with us today to the hotel? We can start tomorrow morning then,' said Vishnu Das.

'That will become four days then. Take her tomorrow.' He said with a rudeness that stung.

Your country could gain independence, your daughters could get an education but when you marry off your daughter you are treated like thieves trying to take away the girl from the in-laws' home. It's humiliating for a girl's parents. Is this the reason why my father never visited me in my *sasural* after my marriage?

Next day, we brought Nutan to the hotel, but we didn't leave for Santiniketan as we hadn't got the train tickets yet.

As soon as Nutan came with us, her demeanour changed. She started talking nineteen to a dozen, showing us the bazaars, the restaurants and all the places she frequented. She didn't utter a word about her husband or her in-laws and I didn't push her.

She was wearing a full-sleeve blouse with her expensive silk saree, something I had never seen her wearing before. It had a high-neck too. She looked smart in it. I thought she was becoming stylish. I didn't know what the blouse was hiding.

Nutan made us stop in front of a *puchka* seller.

'How do you like it, Ma?' she asked before thrusting a *puchka* into her mouth.

The round ball was made of *suji* and inside it was stuffed with boiled *aloo* mixed with tangy spices. It was dipped in tamarind water and served. Inside the mouth, it created a burst of flavours that had the capacity to wipe out all fears and doubts. I guess it did that for all of us.

We returned to the hotel happy. As has been the pattern of my life, happiness is always followed by unspeakable sorrow. I should have been wary.

Nutan was in the bathroom taking a shower. I needed to take out something from one of my travel bags, which was in her room. So I walked in through her unlocked door. I was still rummaging through the bag when Nutan stepped out of the bathroom naked, not knowing I was there.

Although she ran back into the bathroom, that ephemeral peek at her naked body left me shocked. I stood there for a long time not knowing how to react.

What did I just see?

Nutan still had a body that looked like she was a virgin. You might think how do I know that? But don't all women have that instinct? Don't they know the moment the body changes after marriage?

My daughter looked like a sixteen-year-old girl who had never been with a man. And those marks…black round dots all over her hands and on her chest.

I left the room. Nutan emerged dressed in a saree and a long-sleeved blouse. Now I knew why she wore those blouses, to hide the marks. But what were those marks? And why hadn't her marriage been consummated? It was over a year now.

She looked away from me; I didn't have the heart to confront her then. But I slept with her that night with the intention of finding out what was going on.

I very gently broached the topic. I told her I had seen her virgin body. This was a kind of conversation we never had as mother and daughter. But now that I had to have it with her, I had to be careful while approaching the subject. I could make out it was a sensitive issue that I had to talk about delicately.

I started with asking her about the letter.

'There was urgency in the letter that you sent. Is everything okay at your *sasural*, Nutan?' I asked.

Nutan didn't need much prodding. She was an

emotional tsunami waiting to burst out. She started sobbing. I waited for her to regain her composure.

'Even last night, Maji and Bauji came to my room and kept threatening me not to tell you anything. They said I will not be able to go back to that house if I tell you anything.'

'Tell me what?' I was a bit puzzled now.

Nutan suddenly became quiet. She sat on the bed clutching her knees and her head resting on it. Her head was turned to the wall; I could not see her expression.

'Your marriage has not been consummated, right?' I finally asked.

Nutan still didn't look at me, but she gestured a 'No' with her head. I paused to take in the information.

'Why?' I asked.

'He can't, I think…' Nutan's voice trailed off.

'We have slept next to each other for so many months but he has never…'

'Taken any initiative?' I asked.

She moved her head side to side again.

'And if I did…if I did…he would burn me with cigarettes.'

'What? What are you saying?'

'Initially he did it once or twice. But in the months before he left for London, he became a monster. If the tea went a bit cold, he would press the burning cigarette butt into my hands. I would scream but no one would come. If I asked him if I was going to London with him, he would do the same. Sometimes he would pretend that he wanted me in bed and when I took my clothes off, the burning cigarette would come down on my chest, on my back. Uff…Ma, it was so painful.'

I sat there stunned, not knowing what to say. I wasn't prepared for a revelation like this. But I didn't know this was only a small part of my daughter's sufferings.

Nutan wiped her tears. She looked a bit relieved to be able to talk about the pain she had been enduring for over a year.

'So when he said I wasn't going to London, I was relieved. I think he didn't want to take me; that's why his torture had become so unbearable before he left. He wanted to ensure that I would be so afraid that I wouldn't want to go with him. Ma, the Narayan you saw at the wedding and the Narayan I saw every night are two different people. It was like he became a monster at night only to transform back into that suave, good-looking, mild-mannered person in the morning.'

My cheeks were wet now. I felt helpless.

'I had thought that once Narayan left my problems would end but something worse happened…'

'Worse? What happened Nutan? Tell me what happened?'

'I don't know how to tell you, Ma…I don't know how to talk about this.'

Nutan looked down at the bedspread trying to find words. I was wracking my brains, wondering what could be worse than this.

'Your father-in-law…' I stopped mid-sentence

because Nutan was now looking at me with an expression that was a cross between dread and amazement.

'What about my father-in-law?' she asked.

'No, I saw the way you cringed when he touched your head,' I said.

Nutan took a deep breath. 'You saw it right, Ma.'

'Does he torture you too?' I asked alarmed.

'It's a different kind of torture, Ma. The day Narayan left, my mother-in-law came to my room. After a lot of this and that, she came to the point. She told me that since I already know Narayan will not be able to father a child, I should be prepared to have a child with someone else.'

My eyes were popping out of their sockets.

'She told me, *"Beta, ghar ka chirag ayega* (A child will be born). No one will know as long as it is our blood. We will take care of everything."'

'How?'

'She said, "Just keep your bedroom door open at night. Someone will come. Do what he tells you to do and you will have a baby soon".'

'Your father-in-law came?' I blurted out.

Nutan nodded in the affirmative.

'What did he do?'

'I didn't keep my door open. He knocked several times. But I didn't open the door. He called me thinking I would open hearing his voice, but I didn't.'

'But did he finally...?' I asked alarmed.

'No. He hasn't. But I was scared I would not be able

to keep him away for long. In the mornings, my mother-in-law comes and keeps explaining to me why this is the most normal thing to do. And at night he keeps knocking, expecting me to let him in. My mother-in-law even says that they are being decent that he hasn't forced me yet. If I don't relent, he will.'

I cannot tell you how angry I felt. I felt like going straight to their home and throttling Nutan's in-laws. I could not imagine that my daughter was being subjected to this torture.

I blamed myself for becoming ambitious about her future and getting her married at sixteen. If she had still been at home, she would have been safe, protected and happy. Then I thought of Rani. I was fooling myself. Was any place really safe for women?

Next day, we left for Santiniketan. Sitting below the tree and watching my tormented daughter walk around looking so happy and free, just like she had always been, I wanted to give her life back. I wanted to wipe out that miserable one year from her life.

I had lost Rani, I didn't want to lose Nutan. I knew if I sent her back to her *sasural,* she would become like the living dead.

Was I strong enough to find her a light? Was I becoming too ambitious again?

CHAPTER 23

Vishnu Das looked worried and fatigued when he walked into our room at The Grand Hotel. We had returned from Santiniketan that day.

Nutan's revelations had made us so crestfallen that my husband and I were still emotionally coming to terms with the situation that we had pushed our daughter into.

'What did they say?' I asked Vishnu Das anxiously.

'Bauji, did they allow?' Nutan couldn't wait for her father to open his shoes.

'I told them we wanted to take you home and look after you because you have come down with smallpox. Your father-in-law was not willing to believe me. He thought you had told me everything,' said my husband.

'So I have to go back to that place? Nutan looked stricken.

'No, you are going back to Luharu with us,' my husband said.

I heaved a sigh of relief.

'I was very nice to him and feigned that I didn't know anything. I kept telling them how nicely they have been treating my daughter. I told them smallpox is contagious, that is why I did not want you to go there,' he said.

'They believed you that easily?' I asked.

'Not really. Ram Prasad was really suspicious. He came up with subtle threats even. He told me, *'Beti ne paas rakhega to baradari mein naak teri kategi, maahri nahin.'* (If you keep your daughter to yourself. You will be embarrassed, not us.)

'Then how did you convince him?' I asked.

'I carried this with me.' My husband fetched out a piece of paper.

'A doctor's certificate. Where did you get this, Bauji?'

'I have known Dr Satish Chandra Das since I worked in Calcutta. He is a very famous doctor here. I told him my daughter was being tortured and asked for the certificate. He immediately wrote it. With a certificate from a doctor, your father-in-law couldn't do much.'

'You are amazing, Bauji.' Nutan looked at her father admiringly.

Vishnu Das' face clouded. I knew what was on his mind. He knew he hadn't found a permanent solution to the problem. In our community, it was disgraceful for a married daughter to live in her *maika* forever. So would he have to compel Nutan to go back to the hell-hole one day?

I was thinking in the moment. It was important for Nutan to heal first. I wanted her to get over the trauma that her *sasural* had inflicted on her. I wanted her to get back her spotless skin and her effervescent smile.

Now that it was finalised that Nutan was going to Luharu, we were all in a better mental state. I wanted to explore Calcutta a bit before we took the train back home.

'Do you think it's a good idea to go out now? Someone from Nutan's *sasural* might recognise her. And knowing Seth Ram Prasad, he might have stationed a spy in front of the hotel,' said Vishnu Das.

I agreed with him. One wrong step could land us in trouble. So it was better to stay put in the hotel. Such is the situation of women and their parents in our society. It was they who had committed the crime but we were the ones hiding in the hotel like criminals.

Vishnu Das went out to meet his business contacts and returned late in the evening in a better mood. In the morning, I guess his experience at Nutan's *sasural* had left him drained. It must have been an exhausting heckling session that he didn't elucidate to Nutan.

'I have got you something,' he said, taking out some slips of paper from his pocket.

'What is it, Bauji?' Nutan asked with childlike eagerness.

'Both of you always wanted to watch a Hindi film, right? There's one running in a hall right next to this hotel. Kumar is the hero and Madhubala is the heroine. The name of the film is *Amar.*'

'Really? Can we watch it?' I sprang up from the sofa, as if I would walk out of the door right then.

'Yes, I got you the tickets,' he said, handing us three small rectangular pieces of paper. They felt rather thin and limp between the fingers.

Nutan and I kept turning the tickets over and staring at them like we had chanced upon the greatest treasure in the world.

'But when we go, ensure you wear your *ghunghat* drawn to your chest. No way should you be spotted,' he said.

He had got us tickets for the night show that started at 9 pm. The movie hall wasn't that crowded. In fact, there were only a couple of more women in the audience. I guessed 9 pm was no time for even the progressive women of Calcutta to watch a movie.

As we entered the building through a wide grilled gate, two staircases on either side went to the first floor. There was a huge door on the ground floor that led to the seating area but we had tickets to balcony seats. We went up the right stairs and walked in through another huge swinging door.

Then a red-carpeted wide staircase led to the balcony from where we could see the people seated on the ground floor. We sat on the soft and comfortable balcony seats.

Suddenly the huge screen in front of us came to life showing faces of people that were 500 times bigger than our real faces. Nutan and I started clapping like we were watching a feat at the circus.

The first time is always magical and our first movie show was no different. Soon the beautiful Madhubala came on screen. I had never seen anyone as beautiful as her. I had read in a magazine her father lost his job and became her manager. Her career soared but she single-handed earned for her entire family.

I looked at her ethereal face and thought she was a woman whom all of India knew. She was a star. She earned her own money but did she have the independence to spend her own money? Did she get to go where her heart pleased? Do what she wanted to do? Or was she like any other Indian woman – free but not free?

Nutan sat between me and my husband. As the scenes on the giant screen kept her captivated and the light kept dancing on her face, my mind kept wandering to Nutan's bleak future. A divorce was unthinkable in our society. So what was the alternative? Having a child with Seth Ram Prasad and behaving as if everything was hunky dory? And if the first-born was a girl…I shuddered.

It was strange how destiny always found a way to dash a woman's hopes. I had hoped my husband was educated so I would get to go to school. That never happened. Nutan had hoped she would study in a school abroad. That never happened.

We were generations apart, situations apart, but our destinies had a way of colliding. We never got what we hoped for instead we were handed out shame, insult, humiliation.

I kept asking myself: Who was worse, Bhagwani Devi

or Sharda Devi? My mother-in-law never had a façade to maintain but Sharda Devi turned out to be the sweet-talking she-devil who lured a girl into her clutches with her goodness, then at her own sweet will tossed her into the demon's den.

'Ma, did you see the scene?' Nutan was asking me impatiently.

I was staring at the screen, no doubt. But I hadn't really watched the scene because my thoughts had kept me busy.

'I wasn't paying attention,' I admitted.

'Watch the next scene carefully, Ma.' Nutan seemed excited about something.

So I carefully watched the next scene and the scene after that. It was set in a village and a crowd had gathered. Madhubala was addressing the crowd.

My hands became clammy, beads of sweat appeared on my temples. Vishnu Das was also staring fixedly at the screen.

Three of us couldn't have been wrong together. Could we?

CHAPTER 24

'Bhabhi, you can't imagine their plight. These women have nowhere to go. Their families have been notified but they don't want them back. They would live in the ashrams created for such women all their life. They earn Rs10 a month by doing sewing work. They are tired, hungry, hopeless,' said Kishan, in one breath.

Nutan and I were listening intently.

'Let's get some of them to stay in our hostel. They can get an education, they can learn a skill and they can be independent. What do you think, Bhabhi? Can't we give them a home here?' he asked.

'We can. I think using the hostel for these women is a good idea. But will girls from Luharu attend our school if we start it with these girls from the Jalandhar camp?' I asked thoughtfully.

'Then we are thinking exactly in the same way other

people are thinking at the moment. But they are our daughters and sisters whose lives have been destroyed for no fault of theirs. They are paying the price because some political leaders decided to divide the country on religious lines,' said Kishan.

'I think we should discuss this with Vishnu Das since he would be the one to pay for everything. We can start the school as a rehabilitation centre and hostel and we can welcome day scholars from neighbouring areas as well. Then see how it goes,' I said.

'As if one girl coming back home is not enough, my son is planning to get fifty more girls. Their families don't want to take them but he wants to be their saviour. But he doesn't want to marry, have his own sons. Sometimes I feel I should have died before I saw all this,' said Bhagwani Devi, as she entered the room.

She hadn't given up her habit of listening through the windows. We were not surprised that she had heard every word we had uttered while standing outside the room.

Kishan ignored her completely. Nutan and I shared a quick glance, knowing fully well what she was about to say.

'Nutan, I am telling you. No daughter comes back and lives in her *maika*. You have to deal with the situation yourself, we cannot help you. If you stay here, your brothers will not get married, do you want that?' she asked her.

Nutan's eyes had welled up. My fault. I should have whisked her away knowing what was coming. I couldn't bear to see my daughter crying. I could have killed that old woman.

'Maji, this is my house. I will decide if my daughter gets to stay here or not. The boys you are talking about are my sons. Let me think about their future. You go to the *mandir* and do your *kirtan*, don't get involved in this situation.'

Her eyes had narrowed, I had braced myself for the storm when Kishan started laughing. He kept laughing loudly. Maji looked flabbergasted, Nutan's eyes dried up and I was clueless about what he was driving at.

'She has a problem with Nutan…have you told her we are working on a bigger problem here?' asked Kishan, still laughing.

'*Haan! Bera hai* (Yes. Yes, I know)'. You are getting all those 'impure' women to that school of yours,' said Bhagwani Devi.

'That's for later. I am leaving for Bombay tomorrow to get someone else home,' said Kishan.

'*Kaun*? Tell me who?' Maji asked alarmed.

I glared at Kishan. I hadn't wanted her to know but he had spilled it now.

'Sorry, Bhabhi. I couldn't help it. She talks so badly of other women, what will she do when her daughter comes back?'

'Rani! Rani, is coming back?' asked Bhagwani Devi, looking distraught. I had never known that a mother could look so unhappy at the thought of her daughter coming back home.

'*Woh wapas aake key karegi?* (What will she do after returning?) God knows which man she has been with, what she has been doing all these days.'

'Maji!!' I screamed. One word more and I would have probably got violent.

Our search for Rani took a new turn at the movie hall in Calcutta that day. We had spotted her in the village crowd that was standing around Madhubala. All three of us were sure it was her.

But to be doubly sure, Vishnu Das went back to the projector room the next day and requested them to stop at the scenes to know for sure that it was Rani. He met the hall manager and took the address of the production house that made the film.

I had planned to write a letter to them but Kishan wanted to leave immediately since we were now sure she was part of the film.

Destiny has weird ways of showing the way. If we hadn't gone to watch the film that day, which was the unlikeliest thing for us to do at that time considering the circumstances, we wouldn't have known Rani was still alive.

'Ma, do you think Bua will come back?, Nutan asked me as Kishan left for the railway station in the *tonga*.

'I don't know. I can only hope she will,' I said.

'But Dadi will not let her stay here,' she said.

'Dadi doesn't get to decide. You, I, Bauji, Chachaji all want her to stay with us. If she wants to stay with us, she is most welcome.'

Nutan looked thoughtful. She was toying with a book. I knew she was not really reading.

'If Bua comes back and if I stay back, there is a possibility Azad and Bharat will have to bear the taunts all their life. No one will marry them,' said my daughter.

'They are just kids now. Do we need to think that far?' I asked.

I thought of the taunts I faced all through my childhood because of my mother's death at childbirth. Was I creating a similar situation for my sons because I wanted to give my daughters a better life?

I really didn't want to think about all this anymore. I wanted to protect Nutan with all my heart. Shield her from the atrocities she had been facing in her *sasural*.

Every time I stood at the *chhajja* now, I could imagine Rani walking in through the main door and looking up at me. In my mind, she was back home safe and sound.

I waited with bated breath for Kishan to return from Bombay.

CHAPTER 25

I was sitting on a charpoy in the *aangan* chopping vegetables. Azad and Bharat were playing cricket close by and Nutan was swinging on the *jhula* in the corner, reading a book. It was a picture of bliss but who knew the turmoil that was going on in my mind?

It was almost going to be a month that Nutan was in Luharu. We had still not been able to take a decision whether she should go back. If Narayan was a good person, we could have given it a thought. You could still survive terrible in-laws. Hadn't I done that?

Thankfully, Vishnu Das was not a bad human being. But Narayan? Which man burns his wife with cigarettes? If he knew he was impotent, he should not have got married.

Living up to social expectations is so important that if it ruins the life of a girl, so be it. Then I thought about Bhagwani Devi. She was doing the same, wasn't she? She didn't want her own daughter back and now she wanted her granddaughter to go back to her *sasural* despite knowing everything that happened. Daughters were always unimportant, hadn't I known that myself?

Did I, Vishnu Das or Kishan have it in us to protest against that? Would we be able to say that we wouldn't push Nutan into the cauldron of hell? But sending her back would be socially correct even if it burned our daughter her entire life.

I was lost in thought and hadn't noticed that a familiar figure had just walked in through the main door. I got up from the charpoy in a jiffy and looked past him to see if another familiar figure was accompanying him. I ran past him and looked outside, hoping she was standing there to surprise me.

All these years I had painted this scene in my head—my reunion with Rani. It could not be that it would remain just a dream.

'She didn't come, Bhabhi,' Kishan said.

'Why? Why wouldn't she come? Has she become a *Musalmani*?' I blurted out.

'No, she is still a Hindu.'

'Then?'

'She has sent you a letter explaining everything.'

'Chachaji, how did you find Bua? Is she well?' asked Nutan.

'She sends all of you her love.'

'Is she happy?' I asked.

I was in tears now. I sat on the charpoy looking like a wilted tree. All strength had drained away from my body. All these years that Rani was not there and Kishan moved from one refugee camp to another looking for her, every single day I had prayed that we would find her. Now that search had come to an end and yet I was crying alone.

'She lives in a big house near the sea beach,' said Kishan.

'Really? That must be lovely,' said Nutan.

'She works in that house. She looks after two daughters of a widower,' said Kishan.

'...and she works in films too?' asked Nutan.

'I'll tell you everything, let me change and take a bath. It's a long story. But our solace is she's alright. Her employer looks after her well,' said Kishan.

Rani was working in a house looking after kids? Rani, the queen of our household, was a maid? I couldn't believe my ears. She could have come back. Why didn't she come back? By the time Kishan finished his bath, Vishnu Das was already home for lunch. He was upset to know that Rani had refused to come home.

'I am glad to see my daughter is sensible, unlike my sons or my *bahu*. She knows coming back is not an option, so she did not come back,' said Bhagwani Devi, with a smirk on her face.

My mind went back to the day Rani was born. How I had prayed sitting near the bed, for both Rani and Maji to live.

'Kishan, tell us how you found her,' said Vishnu Das,

completely ignoring his mother.

'The address you had given me, I went to that studio first. But Rani's name wasn't there in the list of 'extras': that's what the actors are called who do these background roles,' said Kishan.

'Then what did you do?' asked my husband.

'They told me she was not a regular but when she came to the shooting she came with the producer. They gave me his name and address. I went to his house in a place called Juhu. Rani opened the door when I rang the bell. She was shocked to see me.'

'Was she happy to see you?' asked Nutan.

'Yes, very happy. She started laughing and crying at the same time. She took me inside and made me sit in a very plush sitting room and served me tea. She asked about all of you.'

'How did she go to Bombay? From Luharu to Bombay, it's befuddling!' I said.

'Yes, it is. But on that night, Rani too didn't know where she was going. She has written down everything in this letter, Bhabhi. You can read it out loud.'

Kishan handed me a white envelope. I opened it.

Dear Bhabhi and Bhai,

Please accept my apologies for not contacting you all these years. I didn't know you all were looking for me so anxiously. Trust me, if I had known, I would have got in touch with you. At least l would have let you know that I'm fine. You didn't even know if I was alive or dead. After what I hear from Kishan Bhai,

I feel very guilty for not contacting you.

Actually, so much happened in so little time that I didn't know how to deal with the situation. On the night I was taken away from our Luharu home, I had become unconscious.

I woke up in a small house. My clothes were torn, but there was no blood on them. I could not understand if they had done anything wrong to me. The room was locked and I kept crying sitting in a corner. Then they brought in two more girls and locked them in the same room. The girls were younger than me. They started crying and banging on the door. But no one came to open it.

We were not given anything to eat or drink. I had no clue where I was. Then in the middle of the night, someone opened the door. I couldn't see the person, but I presumed she was a lady. She just told us to follow her to the back door and to run through the field when she opened it. She told us if we didn't run really fast, we would be sold the next day.

The house was totally dark and when she opened the door there was only darkness outside. I felt so scared. But I ran as fast as I could, not knowing where I was going. The two girls followed me. Then we came to a place where we could sense there was a train line and a train was coming. It was a slow goods train, so we jumped up on it. The train was filled with coal and it was pitch black inside.

When we settled down on the floor and our eyes

> *got accustomed to the dark, we realised that it was filled with people. They were so silent that it was impossible to know that there were people inside. I initially got scared thinking they would harm us. Then I realised there were women and children inside too, escaping like us to the unknown.*
>
> *I had dozed off inside the train when I heard the faint cry of a baby. I hadn't even realised that there was a baby on the train till then. Then everyone started saying the baby had to be killed because its cries would bring the mob's attention to the train. I didn't even know at that point if the people I was travelling with were Hindus or Muslims…*
>
> *The men tried to wrench away the baby from the mother's bosom and throw it on the tracks. I can't tell you how traumatic that experience was. I could feel a scuffle taking place. The mother held on with all her strength till she couldn't anymore and the baby was gone.*

I stopped to wipe my tears. Everyone was crying, even Bhagwani Devi.

> *Grown men turning on a baby? What had human beings become? When I think back, I don't know what was more terrible for me. The scene where I remember I was being carried away and Maji was lying on the floor and the guard dead beside her, or this scene where the baby was thrown from the train. I had seen too much in two days.*

We travelled for three days. There was no food or water. The train stopped somewhere. I didn't know then where I was. I was weak and semi-conscious. Through my fading vision I thought I saw some people from the army. Now I know I had jumped on to a goods train that was going to Bombay.

They took us to a large refugee camp that had tents standing in rows, gave us food and water. But I did not have the strength to get out of bed for days. Then a man came to my tent one day and told me if I went with him, I could earn a lot of money. I asked where, he said it was a place called Kamathipura. Later when I asked around, I came to know it was a place where prostitutes lived. While the men kept coming often with lucrative offers, the camp people kept telling us to find jobs because they could not provide us with food anymore.

I thought of sending you a letter many times. I thought of returning home. I wanted you to come and take me away from those tents that got waterlogged when the rains came, from all those men who kept coming up with lewd proposals. I had even written a letter but I never posted it. I will tell you why I changed my mind about returning home.

The two girls who ran away with me stayed in the same tent. One of the girls had registered in the missing women's section in the camp. She was from Serai village which was close to Luharu. She also came from a rich family. Her father came to meet her, gave her money so that she could buy food, find a place to stay, but didn't take her home. He said her two younger sisters would not get married if their abducted sister came back. So she had to make the sacrifice. Her father left. She cried for days.

I then thought about Nutan, Azad and Bharat. I would put you in the same spot if I I came back. Would anyone marry them? I could not let that happen. That is why I did not post the letter.

The camp we were staying in was in a place called Mulund. I started looking for jobs as a maid, cook or nanny. They were taking women for making achar; I registered my name there too. Then they told me a widower was looking for a lady to look after his two small daughters.

I jumped at the opportunity. Moving out of such a filthy camp and getting to live in a proper house after so many months was like heaven. Bhabhi, my looking after Nutan, Azad and Bharat came handy. I turned out to be really good at my job and my employer was very happy. I look after the girls, who are now twelve and fifteen years old, also take care of the needs of my employer. I cook and clean and I won't say I am unhappy.

One day, my employer, who produces films, needed a woman to do a small role and felt that I could do it. He took me to the studio. I gave the shot and the director was happy. From then on, I started landing small roles here and there. That's how you saw me in

Amar. The pay is not too bad and I go to the studio with my employer and come back with him. I have worked with Madhubala, Nargis, Meena Kumari. He doesn't treat me as a maid, neither does he think of making me his wife. He knows everything about me. Knows I am from a good family, but still he hasn't ever thought of marriage with me, despite the fact that I am nothing less than a mother to his children. If I had been married with children it would have been better. A married woman has respect, something I will never have. Although I have everything else. This is my home now. You can come and meet me. But it's best I do not come to Luharu ever again. It would be very painful for all of us.

Love and regards
Yours
Rani

'What did she mean? She is a *rakhel* now?' the words escaped Bhagwani Devi's mouth blatantly.

My cheeks flushed red in embarrassment.

'Don't talk like that, Ma. After all that she has gone through, this is the only thing you can say?' asked Kishan.

'You have understood wrong. She said he could have married her: Has she said anything more?' asked Vishnu Das.

'My sons are like *doodh peeta bacche, kime samajh koni aawey,'* (My sons are like kids, they do not understand anything) she retorted.

My mind was stuck on Rani's last words: A married woman has respect, something I will never have.

Should Nutan then be sent back to her sasural?

CHAPTER 26

Nutan is sitting at the dining table. Yes, we have one now. She is making designs with her soft fingertips on the table top. I am sitting next to her, writing the monthly grocery list.

I glance sideways at her fingers, trying to figure out what she is writing or drawing. She is humming a song too, an old folk number usually sung at weddings. She has a lilting voice but on her lips the melody sounds forlorn.

My eyes keep following her fingers till I realise she is writing something, a word perhaps.

She has written, 'Du….' Then it strikes me.

She is writing *dujjar:* divorcee. I turn my face away to hide the stab of pain I feel in my heart.

In our community, this is probably the most dreaded word. Being a *dujjar* is similar to being an untouchable.

Women wear their *mangalsutras* like medals. This is it. This is what matters. What happens to a married woman behind closed doors does not matter. It is actually irrelevant in the larger scheme of things, as long as she keeps wearing that medal without complaint and keeps bearing male heirs.

'*Dujjar*, your daughter will become a *dujjar*,' Ram Prasad had shouted on the trunk call to Vishnu Das when he talked of ending the marriage.

Then he had laughed. '*Talakshuda beti ne ghar pe bitha ker rakhoge?* (You will keep your divorced daughter sitting at home?) You must be mad. Send her back to her *sasural*. There is going to be no conversation over this.'

My husband had hung up in silence. Then their threats started. Through calls, through letters and through Sunehri Devi, who did everything to provoke Maji to send Nutan back.

Maji also tried her best to convince us. Then she used histrionics and came down to pressure tactics.

'I always told you this haveli only has *manhoos* women. One woman devoured her mother the moment she was born, another got abducted and became a mistress and now we have the other one all ready to become a *dujjar*. Hey Ram!'

'Maji, you know your sons think differently. If anyone has reaped the benefits of Vishnu Das' progressive attitude, it is you. You happily came down to attend Geeta's wedding despite being a widow. When he said the restrictions that a widow has to follow will not be applied in your case, you embraced his diktats with open arms because it worked in your favour. Now when it's about the daughter of this same house, you want to push her back to hell.'

For the first time in my life, Bhagwani Devi's expression told me that she was not framing a comeback in her head. She fell silent. In other circumstances, I would have considered this a victory, but the battle ahead was so big that these tiny wins were insignificant now.

I had thought the battle would be with Nutan's *sasural* but hadn't really thought that we would actually be waging a war against society. The matter with Nutan's father-in-law could only be settled when Kishan went to Calcutta, took the police with him to Nutan's *sasural* and demanded Narayan's medical test report.

Narayan was back in Calcutta at that time and that helped. He convinced his father to get the divorce done. A medical test was definitely not something he wanted to get into.

Seeing Narayan's signature on the divorce papers, Nutan was initially very happy. At that point, she had no clue what lay ahead for her. Sunehri Devi, Narayan's grandmother, had poisoned people's mind in our community well enough and it soon started showing its effects.

One of Maji's charpoy ladies took Nutan aside one day and asked her, 'You used to look at boys from the balcony all day and you now say people in your *sasural* were bad? *Key zamana aa gayahai!* (What has the world become!). You are a spoilt woman yourself and you played with other people's *izzat*!'

'Boys from the balcony...?' Nutan first fumbled, then went red in the face and rushed up the stairs to her room.

From that day on, Vishnu Das stopped Bhagwani Devi's charpoy sessions. But then, you can stop people entering your home but you cannot stop them from talking behind your back. The whispers continued, the rumours spread like wildfire and people started avoiding us.

When I started approaching families to send their daughters to our school, the situation became worse. One lady was blatant enough to tell me, 'You couldn't bring up your daughter properly...she couldn't be happy in such a reputed family in a big city and you will now give *shiksha* in your school to our daughters?'

I kept mum. I had nothing to say.

Meanwhile, Kishan got permission from government agencies to move thirty rescued women from an Ashram in Jalandhar to our hostel. Just before the women were supposed to arrive, a mob attacked the school.

They went on a rampage. 'We won't let you bring these impure women to Luharu,' they shouted.

Thankfully, none of us were in school that day. Beds and almirahs were broken in the hostel, tables and benches destroyed in the classrooms, but no life was jeopardised. I feared that we had ended up recreating the violence we witnessed during Partition by trying to help women who had been affected so adversely by it. Such is the irony of life.

Kishan stalled the arrival of the women from Jalandhar. We stopped going to the school and waited for the frenzy to die down. That's when the worst happened.

Nutan and I left home one day to go to the *mandir*. Nutan seemed to find solace praying to God and I encouraged her. The *mandir* was where I had also gone as a child when I was looking for direction in life.

On our way back, we were tailed by a group of boys. They were in their late teens or even older. They were after Nutan and my being with her did not make any difference to them. They kept hooting at her. As we increased our pace, they increased theirs too.

Who were these boys? Many people had moved into Luharu since Partition; it no longer remained a town where everyone knew everyone.

I didn't know it had slid into such anarchy that a daughter was no longer safe with her mother.

'*Aey dujjar*! (You divorcee)' they taunted. 'Come, we are there to fulfil your needs.'

I felt a chill go down my spine. Nutan had turned ashen and tears were rolling down her eyes. They were getting dangerously close.

A few steps more and we would reach home. The boys were getting really lewd and rowdy.

I pushed Nutan through the main door and closed it after her. I felt if I couldn't stand up for Nutan that day, I wouldn't ever be able to shield her from this cruel society. All my life, I had learnt to take it on the chin and never retaliate. I had followed this principle diligently. But there has to be a time when you have to listen to your inner voice.

I very calmly said to the boys, 'I will come with you. *Chal* (Come), where do you want to go?'

They were taken aback. They didn't expect me to turn back. Women never retaliated. They were not used to being challenged by women.

They were petty stalkers enjoying a power trip harassing a young girl. The moment I confronted them, they became like dogs with their tails tucked between their legs, looking for an opportunity to slip away.

Then I heard the door open behind me and was filled with a sense of dread that Nutan had stepped out too. Something I didn't want.

'I will come with you too,' Maji said as she stepped out of the door.

Maji was standing next to me, her eyes turned to mine reassuringly.

'You called my granddaughter names? Called her *dujjar*? Come, let's go to your house and see what they have to say about this? You must be having sisters, mothers and grandmothers at home. We would love to meet them. Take us with you,' she said.

The boys kept looking at each other. They had been caught off guard. They stepped back slowly. Maji started walking towards them.

They started running.

Back at home, Nutan was trembling.

Maji brought us two glasses of water. Bhagwani Devi serving me water was probably a first in my life.

'When you have chosen this path, you have to learn

to face life,' she said.

I wasn't sure if she would start off another tirade now. I was never sure of what went on in my mother-in-law's mind.

'Nutan, you go upstairs,' I commanded. I could not let her go through more humiliation.

'No, I really mean it. Nutan, you have to be strong; look these men straight in the eye and make them fearful of you,' she said.

I hadn't expected her to support me in shooing away the boys, neither had I expected her to say this.

'From now on, take me along with you always, I will teach these bastards a lesson. They will never dare to do something like this again,' she said.

I guess this is what life is about. When you are down in the dumps, support comes from the most unexpected quarters. Maji had tormented me all my life but at that moment, by showing her support to Nutan, she had absolved herself.

Despite Maji's surprisingly supportive stance and all our efforts to keep Nutan cheerful and positive, from that day she started sinking into a depressive state. She spoke very little, ate even less and rarely played with her brothers.

She stopped talking about the school around which she was building her dream project. If she spoke at all, she sometimes mentioned her wish to join a religious organisation and become a *sadhvi* (female ascetic).

Sitting at the dining table, when she had started

humming a song, I had felt my heart swelling with hope for my daughter only to be brutally crushed the next moment by the realisation of what she was writing with her fingers on the table.

Dujjar! Was this going to be her only identity now, an identity that society had inked on her forehead with an invisible ink so that she wouldn't forget it for a moment? *Baanj, dujjar, rakhel* ...it's always the women!

CHAPTER 27

Five years later...

I am sitting on the *jhula* in the *aangan*. The house is quiet, like it used to be in my childhood. Azad and Bharat don't make a din anymore playing cricket in the *aangan.* My fourteen-year-old twins are engrossed in their books when they are at home; at all other times, they play cricket with their friends in the fields nearby. Meanwhile Nutan...

She is the reason why I am now waiting, decked up in a *tussar* saree with a dark pink border, the pallu pinned with a ruby brooch.

In the last five years, Nutan's personality has undergone as much transformation as mine. Apart from being Vishnu Das' wife and Azad-Bharat's mother, I have another identity. In Luharu, I am known as Badi Ma.

Nutan is Badi Didi. Like a caterpillar weaves a cocoon

to eventually emerge as a butterfly, Nutan has undergone a metamorphosis. There was a time she had sunk into a shell and we were worried she would never be able to pull herself out of it. Thankfully, she has proved us wrong. She did become a butterfly, touching everything around her with her magic wings.

She now wears the name Badi Didi like a badge of honour; no one has heard the word *dujjar* uttered around her for a long time. Through her hard work and dedication, she has banished her identity of a divorcee into oblivion.

'Nutan! Nutan!' I call her from below the *chhajja*. Why is she taking so long to get ready?

Vishnu Das comes down to the *aangan* dressed up in a classy grey *sherwani* and a Gandhi *topi*. His greying sideburns add to his personality. Years of working in the sun at the *Anaaj Mandi* have tanned his face and there are crow's feet around his eyes. However, age hasn't taken away the sparkle in them.

At forty-nine, my husband still has a lithe frame, the sharp nose adding character to his face. I don't know why, looking at him I suddenly remember our wedding day, when I got married to him without even knowing how he looked.

'Nutan is not ready yet? We can't be late, Roheeni. We have to welcome him at the station,' he says.

'*Arrey*! I have been calling her, she's not replying. Let me go up,' I say.

At the bottom of the stairs, I meet Kishan struggling

to navigate the steep steps. His limp troubles him a lot these days but if I extended my hand, I know he would give me a stern look. So, instead of my hand, I gave him my smile, a broad one, which he instantly reciprocates.

'I'm ready,' says Kishan.

'You are saying it as if you are wearing anything different,' I joke. 'It's the same *khadi johor*-coat-*dhoti* you wear every day.'

'Imagine me wearing a *sherwani* like your husband. I would look so ridiculous. I would be taken away to the circus to work as a joker.'

I had never thought that one day, I would be joking with Kishan like this. Our relationship in its initial days had witnessed a lot of hate, confusion and feelings of betrayal but as the years passed by and we got to know each other better, we developed a strong bond of friendship.

Now I can proudly say that Kishan is the brother I always wanted; someone who tries to understand me and stands by me through thick and thin. Without Kishan, today wouldn't have come. Nutan wouldn't have been who she is.

'Of course, Nutan is not ready yet...' he laughs.

'I am going to her room to check,' I say.

I grab the rope and go up the stairs. At forty-one, I am still pretty agile. But it's also true I am no longer the thin bag of bones that sprinted up and down these stairs on her wedding day thirty-three years back. My body carries the scars of extreme hard work, miscarriage, childbirth and fatigue.

I knock on Nutan's door. 'Nutan we are getting late. How long will…' She opens the door and cuts me off mid-sentence.

'I have an eye on the watch, Ma. Stop fretting.'

She is in a beige silk saree with a print of small maroon flowers. Her hair is tied back in a bun, held up by pearl-studded pins. She wears a single string of pearls and a simple pearl bracelet.

'Am I looking good?' she asks me.

I can't say a word. I draw her close and plant a kiss on her forehead.

It's her day. She looks the part. The erudite, go-getter Badi Didi, who takes up challenges like they are an everyday affair, who never went to school herself but built one that is changing the lives of so many girls and women.

Azad, Bharat and Maji have all assembled in the *aangan*. The twins have taken care to dress up like their father, combing their usually dishevelled hair for a change. They are so proud of their elder sister and so excited about the award ceremony that they haven't slept properly.

'Have you ordered rose garlands? He likes roses. You know that, right?' I ask my husband.

'You are asking that now?' he asks me, irritated.

'Of course, I have made all the arrangements.'

He never forgets important things. I am plain nervous, unnecessarily trying to check on things at the last moment.

We walk through the lane to get to the main road where our car is waiting. My husband acquired an Ambassador car recently. It's the prized possession of the whole family.

As soon as we step out of the main door, we see that people of our *mohalla* have assembled in front of their houses. The moment they see us, they start clapping. I can't fight the goose bumps that appear on my arms, my throat feels parched and I keep telling myself I shouldn't start crying now.

It's an unbelievable moment. Nutan looks equally perplexed and emotional. Only a few years back, people in the same lane had closed their doors on her face because she is a *dujjar*. But my daughter has proved that a woman can change her own fate. A woman can decide how society will perceive her.

When the rampage and protests died down, we inaugurated the school with just three students. Nutan became a different person when she entered the school premises. She worked from dawn till midnight to make her dream come true. By the end of that year, we had thirty girls in our school and thirty women from an ashram in Jalandhar had been shifted to our hostel.

Now we have 200 students and the numbers in the hostel keep changing as women come, get an education and develop skills in sewing, printing, cooking and a whole lot of other skills. They leave the hostel after they find a job. In the past five years, we have rehabilitated 400 women who suffered during Partition.

Although we all supported Nutan in whatever way we could, the school was her baby that she built with her sweat and blood.

She made Nutan Balika Vidyalaya the pride of Luharu. That was the reason Nutan is now receiving the award for the Social Activist of the Year.

When we reach the station, it is already brimming with people. It's not every day that India's Prime Minister visits Luharu. People had apparently gathered there since dawn to secure a vantage point from where they would be able to see him.

As the train pulls up, people go berserk as they chant '*Bharat Mata ki jai! Pandit Nehru ki jai.*'

Nutan steps forward to put the garland around the Prime Minister's neck.

Any other day, if you stepped into Nutan Balika Vidyalaya, you would have seen a class in progress under a tree, an idea Nutan had borrowed from Rabindranath Tagore's Santiniketan.

Today, the place has been decorated with paper festoons and flowers. The orange and white walls of the building look beautiful as the backdrop of the national flag that has been hoisted.

The verdant green school ground is where all the chairs have been placed and seating arrangements have been made. The girls are all standing in a queue dressed in starched cotton sarees, hair tied in braids and ribbons and a rose tucked in. Jawaharlal Nehru greets each and every student as he walks around the grounds.

Nutan escorts him, introducing him to the teachers, women from the hostel and other staff members. Then he climbs the makeshift stage.

'I want to congratulate Nutan for her phenomenal work in the area of education for women and rehabilitation of women who have been displaced by Partition. She has shown that if there is a will, there is always a way. Our country needs daughters like her. I want to congratulate her parents for bringing up a daughter that the country is proud of,' says Pandit Nehru.

'I would like to pass on the mike to the winner of the award,' he says.

When Nutan comes on the stage, the applause almost drowns her voice. All those present at the function stand up to convey their appreciation for my daughter. I choke up, thinking of the life she would have had if we had sent her back to her *sasural*—and the life she has made for herself away from it.

Sometimes, destiny has bigger plans and we have to go through fire to fulfil that destiny. Nutan's life, or for that matter, my life, are examples of that.

My thoughts are interrupted by Nutan saying '…I owe my success to my mother. She always wanted to go to school, but that never happened. She learned to secretely read and write from Babba, the priest at our *mandir*. Then she took the initiative to start classes for a few girls like me in the *mandir aangan*. I never went to school either, but she instilled the love of books in me. This school is her dream that I fulfilled. I have gone through endless battles to reach where I am but my mother did not doubt, even for a day, that I would make it. She always had the belief and conviction that I would be able to do it.

'My mother and I had a vision together, but if my father and uncle had not supported us constantly– financially, physically and emotionally, we could have never done it…'

I am not listening anymore. I see her standing behind in the long row of chairs in the middle of the crowd. Some people have spotted her before me. They have already started whispering, 'Isn't that Rani Bala Devi, the film actress?'

She has kept her promise. She has come.

I don't believe in happy endings because you do not really know what the future has in store for you. However, that doesn't mean you don't keep striving.

Life has taught me this valuable lesson.

GLOSSARY

Aangan – courtyard
Aarti – Hindu worship ritual
Achar – pickle
Aloo – potato
Aloor dom – potato dish
Anaaj – grains
Anaaj Mandi – wholesale market to buy and sell grains
Angeethi – earthen stove used for cooking
Angia – blouse worn over the traditional long skirt
Atta – flour
Baanj – woman who is unable to bear children
Bachao – Save me!
Baithak – sitting room for guests
Bapu – Popular name given to Mahatma Gandhi
Baraat – groom's procession to the wedding venue
Bauji – respectful term for father
Bazaar – market
Beta – loving way of addressing a son/boy

Beti – loving way of addressing a daughter/girl
Bhagwan – God
Bua – Aunt (father's sister)
Chadar – woven cotton shawl
Chakki – grain grinder made of two circular stones
Chhajja – balcony
Chor – robber
Chup – Shut up!
Dadi – grandmother
Dai – Midwife/nurse who assists in delivery of babies
Dholak – musical instrument
Dhoti – man's loose garment for the lower body
Diya – earthen lamp
Dujjar – divorcee
Gath Bandhan – Hindu wedding ritual
Ghaghra – traditional long skirt worn by women in Haryana
Ghee – clarified butter
Ghunghat – veil
Gittey – indoor game played with pebbles
Gully – lane
Halwai – caterer, cook
Hartal – strike
Haveli – traditional mansion
Ikka-dukka – outdoor game played by kids
Imarti – North Indian sweet made by deep-frying lentil flour batter in a circular flower shape, then soaking in sugar syrup
Jaali – panel of stone, metal or wood with carvings
Jalwa Pujan – ritual performed after the birth of a boy
Janani – female, woman

Jharoka – big window with carvings in a haveli
Jhola – cotton bag
Jhula – swing
Jinns – mythical, supernatural creatures
Jui Khilai – game played by bride and groom to break the ice
Kaarigar – carpenter
Kadhai – circular deep pot made of iron used for cooking
Kanyadan – wedding ceremony performed by bride's parents
Kataar – sickle
Kesari – saffron
Khaat – cot, bed strung with rope
Khalifat movement – agitation by Indian Muslims allied with Indian nationalists for restoring the Ottoman Sultan
Khatarnak – dangerous
Khoriya – mime dance performed at weddings
Kheer – sweet dish made of rice and milk
Kirtan – devotional songs
Kotha – in Haryana, room within a room for storage and privacy
Krantikari – revolutionary
Kuccha house – house made of mud and straw
Kurta – loose collarless shirt
Kul Devi – deity of the family
Lathi – long wooden stick used as a weapon
Laddoo – round sweet prepared with flour, ghee and sugar
Langoti – diaper
Latrine – toilet
Luchi – deep-fried flat bread
Lukka-chhuppi – game of hide-and-seek

Maika – mother's house
Mandir – temple
Manhoos – inauspicious
Mathadi, bhujia – dry snacks savoured with beverages
Mehendi – henna used to decorate hands for auspicious ceremonies
Mohalla – neighbourhood with houses clustered together
Mooh Dikhai rasam – post-wedding ritual wherein the new bride is seen by relatives and neighbours for the first time and given gifts
Muktidham Ashram – place to retire after renouncing worldly duties
Naala – open gutter
Nuskha – home remedy
Papad – crisp round snack like chips
Pagri – turban worn by North Indian men of superior class
Pani Graham – wedding ritual
Pataka – cracker
Pehredars – watchmen
phulka – *roti, chapati* (traditional Indian bread)
Poorna Swaraj – complete freedom
Pucca house – house of bricks and mortar
Puja – worship
Pujari – priest
Puri – fried *chapati* prepared on occasions and festivals
Rakhel – mistress
Rangoli – art form made with flowers and dry colours on the floor
Rani – queen

Rasoi – kitchen
Rishta – marriage proposal
Sasural – marital home
Seera – desert made with flour, dry fruit and sugar
Shamshan ghat – cremation ground
Sherwani – traditional attire for Muslim men
Shiksha – education
Suji – semolina
Tabeez – auspicious pendant worn for protection from evil
Tai – Aunt (respectful term for any elderly woman in Haryana)
Talwar – sword
Thaapa – wedding ritual wherein a figure is drawn on the wall and worshipped
Thali – big plate
Tehkhana – basement room
Tonga – horse-drawn cart
Tongawalla – driver of a horse-drawn cart
Topi – cap
Tussar – fabric
Vidaai – farewell ritual for the bride by her parents
Vidhwa – widow
Vyapar – business
Vyapari – businessman